raindrips to Rethfernhim series #1

The Lingering Longing for a Long Lost Love

Rosina Plumley

Inconsequential Diversions

Canadian Cataloging in Publication Data
Plumley, Rosina
Editor: Dubey, Rod
The Lingering Longing
for a Long Lost Love
978-1-895166-29-3
1. Fiction. I. Title. II. Series.
Printed and bound in North America.
First published 2018
This edition published in 2022
Published by Inconsequential Diversions

*Humph is in his doge. Words weigh no more to him
than raindrips to Rethfernhim.*
– James Joyce, *Finnegan's Wake*

Excerpts from Gerald Conway's 1946 Journal

Edited by

Rod Dubey

Editor's Preface

This is the first publication of the late Gerald Conway's memoir from 1946. The events it describes were recounted in newspapers of the day and have been repeated and commented on since, but a number of aspects of the story were unknown (until now).

The journal was recently discovered in a shoe box by Conway's grandchild, Rosina Plumley, along with sixty or so photographs stuck between the pages. They are included here.

I don't point out "new revelations", although I do make editorial comments on Conway's credibility since it has been attacked. I have omitted a few passages from the memoir which do not relate to the famous "crime story".

This journal is a social document of post-war America. It was a period characterized by economic expansion, the beginning of the atomic age, the Cold War, labor unrest, the last hurrah of a radical labor movement, and new technology.

I speak somewhat to these throughout and to the human damage suffered by those who survived two wars (which is central to the events the journal describes).

The Red Scare, McCarthyism and mass immigration added to the anxiety and paranoia about others brought about by propaganda during the war, the loss of the reality people knew, and the growth of the surveillance state. The post-war proliferation of advertising, mass media, and imagery expanded an ontological crisis marked by uncertainty of the other, the death of reality, noir, and the advance of spectacle and simulation.

This is a story set in, on, and around trains. There is a dislocation from a known community (geographically and socially) on a train where we are uncertain of others and if moral norms persist. It could be said that the train functions as a metaphor of the time that was being ushered in.

The growing uncertainty regarding reality was also the case with the crime itself. Conway's initial questions about whodunit, acting like a pre-war detective in trying to understand the reality of who was responsible for what he'd seen occur, eventually turns to questions about the nature of what he saw and whether the attack was even "real".

Rod Dubey

The iconic photograph of Charlotte Wyndham is from 1880. I've heard it said that the photo was taken following a suicide attempt after her young man died. Apparently he'd decided against taking any sort of treatment for some illness;

appendicitis I think.

Although I know death from it was not uncommon at the time, my understanding is that treatments for the well-to-do were becoming available, and I'd heard that, like Charlotte, he came from a well-off family.

The story was that he'd rejected his parents' life to live an austere existence in a cabin. In any case, he died soon after. Death from a resistance to modernism I suppose you could say or to a rejection of privilege.[1]

____

1 None of this interpretation may be correct. Charlotte's lover was Hugh Manners. His views are unknown. One of his nieces however, Louisa Manners, became a sort of celebrity before "The Great War". In spite of her efforts at anonymity, Louisa's decision to stop reading newspapers, got around. She gained fame for it. This was a newspaper piñata, beaten for the treats it delivered in the form of opportunities for the print media to scoff at any radicalism which challenged their importance and acumen.

It was early September, 1946. We were gathered at an event staged by the railroad to thank their employees who'd served during the war.

We stood cheek by jowl in a rented hall, squeezing together front and center for a better look at novelist Charlotte Wyndham, the special guest. She would have been 84 or so by then. She was striking. There was an intelligence in that face – or did I imagine it because she was illustrious?[2] It occurred to me that because of the famous photo of Wyndham – who was purported to have had many lovers over the years – she might always be the sad, lonely Victorian in the popular mind, in spite of all evidence to the contrary.

The old lady was there to receive a check from K&L Rail majority owner, John Spires; a large donation for her charity

____

2 Aren't revolutionaries always beautiful, regardless of age or gender?

to support the orphans of servicemen who'd died in the war.

"Spires is trying to buy some guilt relief," a young man who I was jammed up against said to no one in particular.

"Shh!" responded a wealthy looking woman – who I didn't recognize as an employee – "he doesn't feel guilty because he's got nothing to feel guilty about."

"Urging Truman to intervene in a democratic strike to crush it!" the man countered. "Maybe you're partly right though. He won't feel any guilt."

The woman gasped. Others pretended not to have heard.

After the check presentation, us demobilized vets gathered up front to receive ribbons and listen to speeches from the executives of the company.[3]

There may have been a certain irony in Charlotte Wyndham accepting money from a wealthy railroad mogul. Based on her novels, her politics would probably have been at the opposite end of the spectrum from those of John Spires.

____

3 Of the approximately 16 million U.S. service people active during WW2, nearly 400,000 died and almost 700,000 were injured. The statistic that can't be calculated is how many millions upon millions had their lives shattered by the previous statistics. (And this of course says nothing of the tens of millions who died, were injured, and affected, around the world.)

And railroads – assuming Charlotte Wyndham shared the views of her dead lover concerning modern life – were particularly important in bringing about the world he'd died resisting.[4]

Trains were instrumental to the industrial revolution. They must have been a gross affront to the calm and quiet of the pre-industrial countryside. I think of the 1844 image of a steam engine painted by JMW Turner on behalf of the railways. (Nature – in the form of a foreground rabbit – had better get out of the way!)

The demands of business for speed and power eventually made steam engines quaint relics; trains always being a

---

4 And given the self-sustaining life she led at her "Utopian compound" (as it was called) it seems strange she would have accepted charity at all (although it was likely a compromise on behalf of the orphaned children).

reflection of technical innovation that expand our world, trade, our experience of and connection to others.[56]

____

5 One could say more about the effects of trains … such as the blasted scar they made on the land, movement as a straight line instead of following the land, the changing perception of distance, changing people's relations to their neighbours and land, and the new rhythm of travel.

6 On the other hand, few things have been as destructive to humanity as the railroad. For example, there is the devastating environmental damage set off by the increased mining and distribution of coal. Railroad tracks and the linking of towns to the rail system had a destructive effect on communities and farms. With the movement of goods and people, our reliance on commodities increased as people's autonomy waned. An attendant increase in social isolation and fear of the other followed. Wars gained in ferocity and scale. And there is the argument that WW1 was primarily caused by the railways. German industrial growth led to their expansion of rail lines to the east, which threatened imperial interests, and their schedules allowed for the amassing of armies.

I think it would be fair to say that trains still encapsulated the state of the world and reflected its changes. They continued to be socially and culturally significant.

Thanks to its employees, railroads had just helped us to win a war by carrying raw materials, finished goods and soldiers around North America and Europe.[7]

And railroads even manifested the modern class divide, as

7 Any attribution of nobility to trains is misplaced as they were also used by Nazi Germany. One particularly thinks of the millions upon millions transported in cattle cars as forced labor or to extermination camps.

I'd just heard it expressed by a young man. Their unions were among the nation's most powerful while the railroad owners were wildly wealthy, and at the center of politics and the economy.[8] The train robber was, not surprisingly, considered by many to be a social bandit and folk hero.[9]

---

8 Marx singled out trains as the primary reason for the solidarity among unions.

9 Railroads were the first huge American companies and ushered in the era of corporate power and influence, and the concentration of wealth. Railroad owners epitomized the Gilded Age robber baron. They were the source of multiple scandals, practiced bribery and the dispensing of graft. They owned politicians who pioneered the turning over of public funds and lands to private interests, the expropriation of acreage from small landholders, the dispensing of government grants, subsidies and legal exceptions, and the granting of monopolies. The unsavory word "railroaded", meaning legislation rammed through without due consideration, entered the lexicon, coming to be used for any legal change instituted without democratic oversight. The American labor movement arose largely in response to the railroads' power, and the latter's control over government.

I was a 26-year-old structural engineer working for the railroad – my education completed before I enlisted. In some ways I was the antithesis of Charlotte Wyndham because I embraced the modern world and the railroads.

There were some who said we had entered the age of the automobile and the airplane, but I wasn't so sure that the railroad hadn't begun a whole new life.[10] The new passenger trains in particular. They were lightweight, high speed, and aerodynamic; the triumph of design, materials, and of giving people what they wanted. The new trains catered to people who'd developed a taste for travel since the war, but travel that allowed them to relax in comfort while watching the world going by.[11]

The trains encapsulated a new romance and glamour of their own. The person on the move, the hero of the novel, the model photographed in the latest fashions, were all situated aboard or near the new trains (and sometimes running along the tops of them in the case of the action hero).[12]

---

10 This seems more like wishful thinking than anything else; to insist on still calling this world "modern" since it was undergoing drastic changes and the end of its grand narrative.

11 Unfortunately the engineering advances attributable to railroads are not explained here but they have obviously been immense, involving infrastructure, energy, hardware, systems, and economics.

12 Elsewhere, the author also seems to imbue older trains with a sort of romanticism (which could be said of his "modernism" in general). In these cases trains appear as a rejection of the new, of the automobile and of the airplane specifically. This may happen with all old technology as it becomes associated with an older nostalgic and familiar world, but it might also be an indication that technical innovation always introduces new complexity, new social problems, a loss of personal and local independence, and more slavery. Conway also romanticizes the countryside, reflecting a sense of loss. Note: bandits also ran across the tops of trains, the fascination with people in danger being democratic.

The ceremony concluded, John Spires walked to the side of the room to receive a painting from a fourteen-year-old girl, daughter of one of the vice presidents.

Spires was impressed with the piece. All smiles. Appropriately, it was a painting of a locomotive done in the style of turn of the century geometric modernism, depicting the beauty of a perfectly functioning machine.

I know little of art but it doesn't surprise me that the train remains a reflection of changing artistic views and a cultural symbol. Hadn't the engineered machine come to possess a sort of beauty; of steel, motion, and raw power? At times, the embodiment and promotion of the ideology of progress, speed and growth.

The crowd dispersed, people grabbed drinks, private conversations started up.

I watched my traveling companion Ted with his charisma and hearty laugh blend with the crowd as he always did.

I was about to pick up a drink when distracted by strained voices several feet behind me. The speakers were attempting to maintain the volume of whispered speech while obviously arguing.

The bold young man from the ballroom was being discretely held by two large specimens, railroad managers who I recognized, not thugs, and who were obviously displeased. Each had an arm.

The young guy – who wore a ribbon on his chest – looked from one to the other and unsuccessfully tried to pull away, first left, then right.

"Let's take a little walk outside," said one of the men, "so we can discuss your views in the detail they deserve."

"Piss off," the young guy whispered to the men.

"Show some class," said the other captor. "We don't want to upset any guests."

Together the threesome began to move, although the young man's legs remained stationary.

I walked around them and stepped in their path.

"Gentlemen," I said softly, "please."

"Excuse us sir," said one of the big men, frowning.

I don't like bullies and felt a camaraderie with the ex-soldier, but took a different tact. "I don't think this is going to do our relationship with the unions any good."

"He's a mouthy little prick," one of the men explained.

"A commie," added his pal.

They moved a bit to their left. So I moved to my right.

The bruisers glowered.

"This is not the time, or place," I added. "He's a veteran."

We all suddenly awakened to the surrounding silence – apart from some far off voices.

We had become the center of attention at some point.

One of the men looked over his shoulder. I followed his gaze and noticed that even our host had paused to watch us.

The big men grumbled and let go of the young man's arms,

more or less pushing him into me.

He looked me in the eye but said nothing as he continued past, and I presume, out of the room.

I glanced toward John Spires, who nodded appreciatively, and I noticed Charlotte Wyndham standing beside him and also looking my way.

May 23, 1946 newsreel: Rail Strike Paralyzes Entire U.S.

"Frantic travelers jam the stations of the nation as the long awaited railroad strike enters its first hours and tickets are no longer to be had.

Weeks of negotiation proved fruitless, cutting off shipments of vital supplies and leaving thousands stranded in every part of the country.

In Washington, storm center of the labor controversy, Colonel Monroe Johnson, Defense Transportation Chief, takes over the railroads with his group of assistants, while at the White House, A.F. Whitney and Alvin Lee Johnston arrive for last minute negotiations with the President's mediators. Railroad management representatives also seek to avert the strike which costs the nation's carriers $25 million daily in lost revenue.

The wheels of the country's railroads grind slowly to a halt as 250,000 trainmen and engineers walk off the job. The nation's main arteries of transportation are cut and America's march toward reconversion suffers another crippling setback."

The angry young man was obviously a strong union supporter. The feelings he'd expressed earlier were the residue of a national railroad strike that concluded a few months earlier.

In 1946, the war had just ended and the official "no strike" policy of union leadership was over – not that there hadn't been plenty of wildcat strikes during the war. I'd heard it explained that people who had fought in the war expected something more from life. In addition to wage issues, they refused arbitrary treatment and bullying. So the country was swept by official strikes.

When the railroad unions went on strike, the government took over the railroads. Truman threatened to bring in the army and to draft union members. He treated strikers as revolutionists and traitors, likened them to the Japs who'd bombed Pearl Harbor, said the strike was an attack on the government, and used powers in a labor dispute that no President had ever dared use. Not surprisingly, the strikers backed down.[13]

------

13 Of course all of this is in line with the history of the West, where the powers that be invoke the language of war whenever it might serve the purpose of making their political opponents into traitors. Ideology loves stupidity in its followers. It helps to kill unions or whoever the "enemy" of the day might be, driving people against things that might even be to their benefit.

Maybe Truman was right in one way. It sure felt like working people could have taken over the country if they'd wanted to.

I wasn't opposed to unions in principle, unlike many other managers. Unions advanced the interests of the railroad as far as I could see. People with some spending money wanted to travel and to buy the products we could bring them.

I wandered through the party, soon realizing that I could no longer see Ted. I was fairly certain where he'd gone. Perhaps not the location, but I knew who he was with.

He was having an affair with Maxine Stiles, wife of our employer. She was twenty years her husband John's junior.

It seemed to me that the affair was pretty brazenly out in the open. This moment being a good example of that. I didn't know how John couldn't see what was right in front of him. And for the hundredth time, wondered if maybe he did.

Ted and I both worked out of the freight yards, offices and roundhouse in the city of Briggs, a couple of hours away.

We'd met in the military. I wasn't an overly social type so he mostly led and I mostly followed. Before we went overseas in '44, we'd spend time at the dances and go around with the girls who lived near the camp. They worked in the train yards and lived in dorms. We spent a lot of time in the common room of those dorms over a period of seven or eight months.

Women were still Ted's primary focus. He was a handsome man, clearly, with a nice head of hair. Even slickum couldn't keep down the thick waves that had grown out since our army days. Big smile with lots of his white teeth showing. It was the smile and the energy even more than the looks that attracted women to him I think.

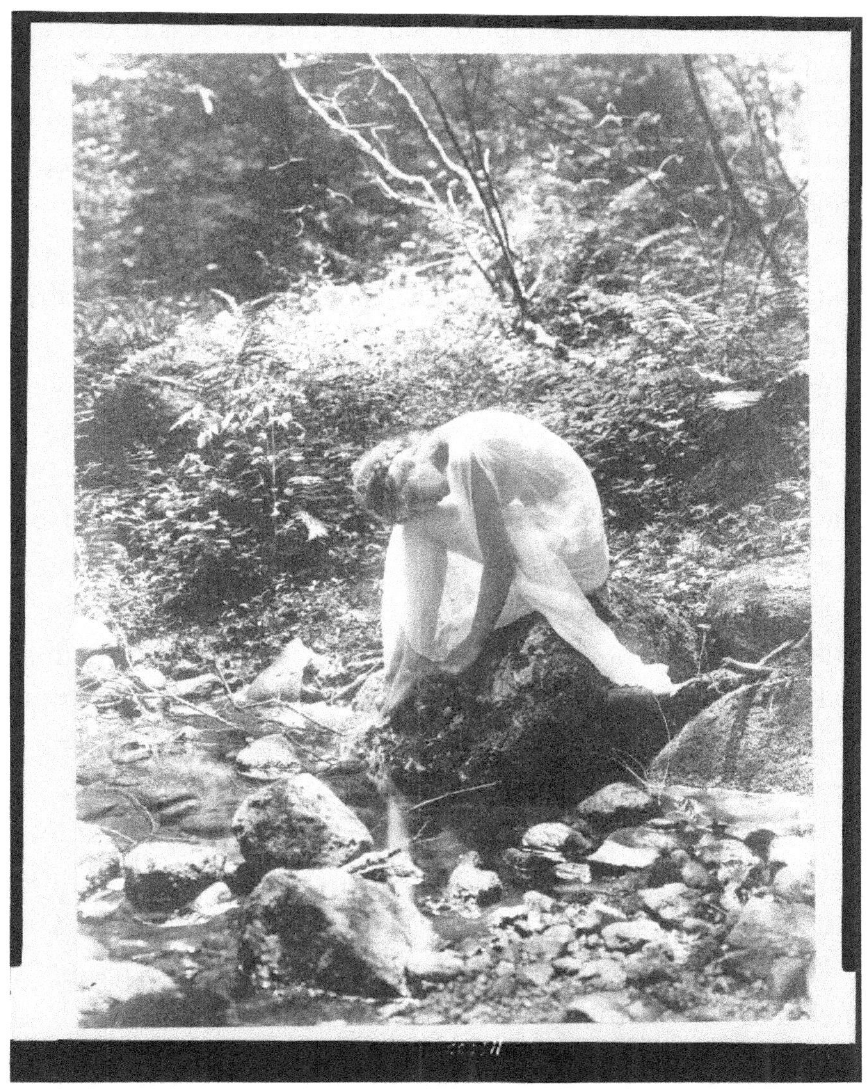

"You're so mysterious," said Victoria, who had taken hold of my arm while pushing her face close to mine. "So quiet."

"Quiet" wasn't something that had ever occurred to me to be an attractive quality.

This was later that same evening, back at Spires' mansion where we were to spend the night. We usually stayed there but on this night, with a lot of senior management in town, it was a surprise we weren't at a hotel. The invite was Maxine's doing, according to Ted. John Stiles had slipped away after the function for a week of out of town business meetings, meaning that Ted and Maxine now had the run of the place.

I was immensely interested in Victoria, the 20-year-old daughter of the Spires. We'd become friends over three previous occasions when I'd stayed at the house. She was interested in the world, the new, and was somewhat Bohemian – I don't know how else to put it.

We began to converse and drifted off to a quiet corner. At one point, apropos of something or other, Victoria went off and returned with several photographs that she said she'd like to show me. They were shots of herself and other women in white or diaphanous gowns. She was obviously proud of them. Some of the photos were of her alone and in others the women were dancing. They looked like they were enacting a Greek drama.

I said, "Some of these individual shots remind me a bit of Julia Margaret Cameron photos; poetic, and the people look like historical figures."

"Well, in a way I guess but the photographer wasn't really after that sort of thing. Cameron was imitating painting,[14] so following certain conventions, whereas photographers today are more interested in breaking the rules and finding out what is unique about photography. Like with these photos. No one is posing the way they are in the Cameron photos. The lines of the bodies aren't controlled since the women are constantly moving, and the lighting isn't controlled. Photography can capture movement. It's like the eye but it isn't.

---

14 Especially the Pre-Raphaelites.

"My friend Pearl is the photographer. She took photos of women at work making planes and tanks during the war, and liked depicting strong independent women so much she decided to keep doing that. These photos are of women exploring what they can do with their bodies and how they can interact with other women's bodies. She does other work too. I like how in some of her photos she parodies or criticizes models, fashion photography, and advertisements that depict women as frail clothes horses or as mousy housewives."

I admired the photos. There was a definite daring quality to a few and I wondered if her parents knew about them.

"Do you show these to many people?"[15]

"Ah, you mean the sensual aspects. No, in fact, you're the first. Keep them, they're a gift. The sensuality is important for Pearl. She recognizes that being able to express that openly is part of the new ability of women to move beyond the limits to their individual freedom that society has always placed on them."

____

15 Conway manifests a degree of prudishness at other times as well, but consistent with the norms of 1946.

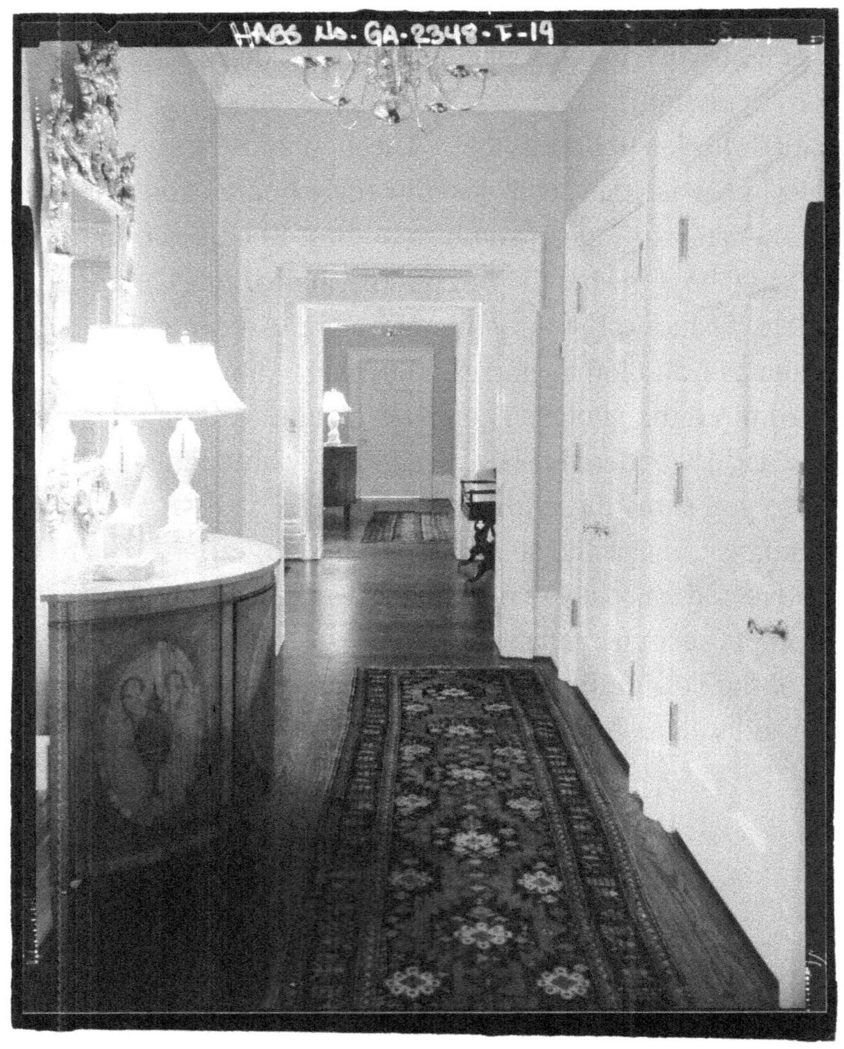

One by one the guests left after dinner. The few staying overnight eventually went off to bed, including Victoria.

Maxine and Ted's eyes had been communicating overtime and they left as well.

Alone, I had a final drink and went to bed.

Approaching the doorway to my bedroom, at the end of the

deserted upstairs hallway, I noticed that the door of the room stood open a few inches.

As I reached for the knob, Victoria's face appeared around the door.

She took hold of my arm and gently pulled me forward. "I have something to show you," she whispered.

Next morning, after breakfast, Ted and I brought our bags downstairs, ready to leave for the train station. It was then I discovered that Maxine was coming with us, for a "shopping trip". I assumed this was spontaneous, so wondered if her husband knew of it.

There was to be a fourth party as well: Charlotte Wyndham. She'd spent the night at the house of a friend who was bringing her to the station.

That was interesting news. I hadn't a clue what I'd say to her, or if I'd have the nerve to say much of anything. But I knew that Ted would be distracted by Maxine so there was a good chance of being compelled to overcome my shyness out of politeness. I'd read most of Wyndham's novels and was pleased I'd at least be able to tell people about having met her.

The train was a small one, put on for the returning railroad people. There weren't as many people aboard as I'd have thought. Many had probably gone home the previous evening.

Ted and Maxine took side by side seats so I sat beside Charlotte Wyndham.

Five months earlier a "war novel" by Charlotte Wyndham had been published and was met with controversy. She hadn't glorified our troops or manliness in the fashion of post-war self-congratulation. How dare she, it was said. More restrained voices had called her the "anti-Hemingway".

The novel is set in southern Italy during WW2 – you may have read it – and tells how the people of a village helped the

Americans against the fascist forces of Mussolini. They were traitors of course, but the Americans didn't judge them for that. It was understandable. We were preferable to living under fascism. But the Americans assumed the villagers were their best friends and must share the same beliefs; that the actions of the locals had affirmed this. The Americans used the town for some post-war propaganda newsreel pieces and set up their regional post-war base there.

But then the villagers asked the Americans to leave. It was a baffling request. How could this be? The townsfolk supported American ideals, didn't they?

When the Americans didn't leave, their base became subject to repeated attacks. Power lines were cut, buildings were burned, and there were many smaller acts of sabotage.

That the villagers – allies of the Americans – could be responsible was hard to believe. But they were. Their alliance with the Americans had just been a temporary one. After the fascists were gone and Mussolini was hung upside down by his ankles in a traditional form of folk justice to show that power had been inverted, the villagers just wanted the Americans to go home and leave them alone. They apparently preferred to remain in their old world and were opposed to incursions regardless of who it was.

What outraged people in America was that the author seemed to be clearly on the side of the "ungrateful" villagers. The author's bias was un-American – some people said – backward, a rejection of America's world leadership. She even depicted Americans striking out at the villagers who'd helped them.

As an ex-soldier, it seemed perfectly understandable to me that people would want to manage their own country. I thought the book showed how propaganda dulled our perceptions, made us jingoistic, arrogant and submissive; that we saw but never understood those people in the lands we marched through.[16]

---

16 The novel is now usually regarded as an attack on the occupation of Italy beginning, in the south, with the surrender in 1943. This has been described as a form of American imperialism that re-instituted elements of fascism – even giving its architects new jobs to combat the possibility of peasant autonomy – so the peasant resistance to American occupation was a continuation of their fight against Mussolini. This interpretation of the novel didn't occur until some modern scholars pointed out what happened after the war in various locales (see, for example, the interview of Noam Chomsky by David Barsamian in *Secrets, Lies and Democracy*, Tuscon: Obidian Press, 1994.)

Charlotte Wyndham was very affable and at ease, commenting on the weather and the inconsequential.

I replied, but I wasn't very good at small talk. "I enjoyed your last novel," I said, "as did my late sister Alice."

Charlotte Wyndham smiled. "You don't have much company in that. You said, your "late" sister. The book only came out recently so I will offer my condolences on your loss."

"Thank you. You gave her some pleasure in her short life so I appreciate it."

There was a long quiet.

"She committed suicide three months ago," I said.

Charlotte shook her head. "How tragic."

Too late I remembered the famous photo of Charlotte when she was young and the story that she had tried to commit suicide. Would it appear I was fishing and had brought up Alice for that reason? I felt that I should make clear I was only speaking about what had happened with my sister.

"Yes. It's always there in my thoughts. I feel like I should have seen it coming but I wasn't living with her. My parents had moved the family out of the city so my father could take a new job. They bought a house in the country. Alice left behind a boyfriend in the city and was angry about having to move. She accused my parents of moving just to break up her romance. There were fights about her visiting the city. My parents didn't want her unsupervised there. Then one day Alice hung herself from a tree in the yard. What I continually wonder about," I said after a short pause, "is if Alice was punishing my parents for the move, by destroying herself. It astounds me that someone could do that, forfeit their life to make a point and to punish their parents. Now her body decomposes in a coffin in a bleak cemetery. Over and over I wonder if people cannot understand the consequences of suicide or if they just become so consumed with striking back that they don't care?"

"But it doesn't sound like you really know that to be her motive. Maybe," Charlotte said, "she was just that unhappy."

Of course I knew she'd been unhappy but it had never occurred to me that this in itself would be sufficient motive for suicide. "I suppose …"

"I don't think you will ever understand what she was feeling because you can only see her with older eyes. You always will. In fact, as you get older you will possibly think about it more and more, and be even more confused. Remember that the young have no sense of the gravity of things, that what is small potatoes for you can be tragic to a fifteen-year-old. The love they feel is always the greatest love ever felt and eternal. If the suicide was an act meant to communicate, maybe she wanted to prove that her love for the young man was real, was a great love that she couldn't live without. Romeo and Juliet. Or maybe she didn't die of a broken heart but by trying to prove she was grown up and that her feelings mattered."

I was told the train would soon stop at Cardew Station, a tiny and largely unused station outside of the city. Passenger trains no longer stopped there.

"We'll get off there because Charlotte lives nearby," Ted said. "We can get a taxi home and drop her, and the woman who's meeting her, at their place."

It suited me. The downtown station was ten miles from Cardew whereas my rooms were only about two miles away; by the rail yards at the edge of the city.

The station began immediately at the conclusion of a bridge which went from rocky high ground to rocky high ground, straddling an arm of Lake Cardew. The station's platform began where the track reached solid ground again.

With the help of the conductor, our luggage was deposited on the platform in front of the small station house, near the end of the bridge.

After disembarking, we milled about, stretching our legs,

while Ted explained that we needed to make our way down a flight of wooden stairs to the parking lot under the bridge. He would flag or call a taxi from there.

Charlotte mentioned that the friend who was meeting her seemed to be late but Ted told her it was no problem, that we would wait downstairs with her.

The train started up and moved forward.

Ted and I each picked up a couple of suitcases and the four of us headed for the wooden stairs.

A man arrived on the platform behind us. I assumed that he too had gotten off the train and I didn't pay him much notice. His back was to me when I glanced in his direction. Not someone I recognized. As we walked toward the stairs, he kept behind us.

I heard him start to whistle *Casey Jones* as we began to descend the stairs. He followed us down.

Ted and Maxine were in front while Charlotte and I trailed. She held the handrail and went very slowly.

After we'd gone down three or four stairs the man trailing began to softly sing *Casey Jones*.

Suddenly he was right behind me and I felt his breath on my neck as he sang directly into my ear:

"Mounted to the cabin with his orders in his hand
And he took his farewell trip to that Promised Land."

I turned my head, annoyed, but the guy brushed past,

taking the stairs three and four at a time. I watched his back and when he got to the sidewalk he sprinted off.

It was very puzzling behaviour. I took two more stairs before it sank in. It may make no sense that I understood something so obscure, but I did.

I dropped the bags and practically picked up Charlotte as I clambered down the steps while yelling to Ted, "Take cover! Take cover!"[17]

With the reflexes of a soldier, Ted didn't hesitate. He hustled Maxine down the final stairs.

The four of us had just rounded the stone containment wall at the foot of the stairs when the explosion occurred. The ground shook. We backed against the wall.

All around us, on both sides of the overhead tracks, it rained burning chunks of wood. And then it snowed charred clothing.

I poked my head around the stone wall and saw that the wooden stairs were completely obliterated. There was just a big empty space.

I scrambled up a steel ladder attached to the final bridge support.

Once I was up top I saw that the rails were intact but the station house was in flames. The door was blown off. Flames were visible inside and licking through the windows.

I could feel the intense heat as I ran forward. I was about to

____

17 That the author understood such an obscure warning does indeed seem unlikely, but the resultant suggestion, made by some, that the author was involved in what happened, because he acted as he did with seemingly no warning, is contradicted by later revelations.

go through the door when a hand gripped my arm.

"Don't," yelled Ted, who'd followed me. "There's no one in inside."

"How can you you know that?"

"The station's closed. Unmanned. We just keep the lost and found luggage here. I arranged the stop here, remember. We were the only ones to get off."

Back on the ground, clothes, apparently from the lost and found luggage, lay scattered all about.

I will always remember the poignant sensation of seeing them. It made the explosion feel like a violation of people's lives, clothes being such personal things, giving it a dimension that simple property damage couldn't.

On Monday morning, as I did every morning on my way to work, I walked past the newsstand near my rooms.

I didn't expect to see any newspaper coverage of the explosion. No reporters had shown up and, after we spoke to the police, we'd gone home. I, for one, still hadn't been contacted by the press.

I was shocked to see the headline: "Attempted Retribution?" I grabbed a copy of the paper, sat down and read of the reporter's impression that the police felt the explosion had been the work of railroad union members – "likely stirred up by communist agitators" – seeking revenge for how their recent strike had been crushed. The idea would have never occurred to me.

As I walked to work I thought about the contention and decided it was a dubious one. The police, press, and politicians, seemed to blame the unions for all life's problems. Of course there was residual bad will after the strike, and Spires was hated by some for having been in there pushing Truman to use his muscle to keep the railroads running, but the strike was over. There'd been an agreement in the end, a gun to the head negotiation for sure, but it was in the past. It wasn't as if a bunch of union men had been shot by troops during the strike and vengeance was being called for.

And besides, what was blowing up a little, unused and deserted rail station past the edge of town going to achieve? The newspaper and the police hadn't said. Other than a bit of expense to rebuild the building, there was no reason that I could think of.[18]

In spite of everything I decided not to rule out the idea of union involvement. Maybe there was evidence of it.

____

18 Of course the 1946 nation-wide strikes precipitated new laws which have crippled unions in the U.S. ever since. Union bureaucrats used the legislation's anti-communist provisions to expel not only communists from leadership but leftists who opposed them, thus ensuring an even more timid union bureaucracy (which, it has been said, was the intention of the law). As we've seen over and over, governments promote the idea of something as a threat in order to expand or hold on to power. Perceived threats are then used to justify the curtailment of civil liberties and the increase of surveillance. For the sake of "safety", fear and hate of some enemy are encouraged so that people will readily submit to more government control and less personal freedom. Communists were the new bête noire, supposedly expanding outward on a quest for world revolution and domination. What was to legally befall unions in the next year might have actually been cause for real anger but, of course, no one then knew for certain what would happen in the future. And if they had known, it would just as likely have been union management who was targeted.

My office was in a building beside the roundhouse and railroad shops. As a structural engineer, I worked on the design and building of rail lines, bridges, and other infrastructure. Railroads were pouring big money into expansion and new sleek trains – called streamliners – that catered to the growing demand for passenger travel.

Rail lines now wove their way across the nation. They were the arteries that provided its lifeblood. Towns and businesses flourished where stations were built; the train shaping the country and holding it together.

Every person who boards a train, legally or not, has a story. No wonder trains feature so prominently in folk songs and film.[19]

From my window at work I could see the yards. When I first began my job, immediately after the war, there were still a few men camping near the tracks.

During the Depression though, in the thirties, hobo camps had lined these tracks, filled with men crisscrossing the country looking for work. What a sad sight that must have been. They had left homes, families, lovers. Or they had lost their homes and the people they loved.

At least they found shelter and some camaraderie around the trains.

The number of tramps lessened with the war. Suddenly, there was work for the older ones and many of the young men joined the rail cars full of troops off to fight. Many never returned.

The railroad is the scene of millions of partings, meetings and reunions every day. Tragedy and joy. If the quintessential story is still the one that comes from the Greeks, where after a voyage of discovery someone returns home transformed, the train is at the center of the modern version. And the Depression and the war were central to many of these sagas.

---

19 This fact could have been developed considerably. *Casey Jones* is a part of this. A Wikipedia entry lists over 1000 popular American songs about trains and this only includes those where they are the primary subject so it could be much longer. E.g. For Tom Waits, a recent addition, they include *Train Song, 2:19, Down There by the Train, Downtown Train and Whistlin' Past the Graveyard*, but not songs like *Ruby's Arms* about a brokenhearted man going off – to WW2? – on a train. "The hobos at the freight yards, have kept their fires burning, So Jesus Christ this goddamn rain will someone put me on a train, I'll never kiss your lips again or break your heart."

I think that the people and stories one finds on a train, anywhere in the world, give the measure of that country. Since trains are synonymous with both luxury and poverty, the variety of stories they contain are vast.

Editor's note: It can be noted that trains were historically significant in U.S. history in less auspicious ways as well. The building of nation-wide railroads in America, for economic and colonial purposes, was characterized by the killing and corralling of native people (demonized, as people defending themselves from pacification, invasion and occupation always are), the destruction of their food sources and culture, the exploitation and murder of Chinese and immigrant workers building railroad lines, the funneling of government money to an assortment of crooks, the facilitation of the spread of religion, the destruction of local economies, and massive land theft, i.e. the happy spread of civilization.

Shooting buffalo from a train was referred to by Harper's Weekly as "a sport that is peculiarly American." This "sporting" slaughter actually had an important role in the genocide of aboriginal people.

"The Transcontinental Railroad made Sheridan's strategy of 'total war' [ed. against native people] much more effective. In the mid-19th century, it was estimated that 30 million to 60 million buffalo roamed the plains. ... The devastation of the buffalo population signaled the end of the Indian Wars, and Native Americans were pushed into reservations. ... By the end of the 19th century, only 300 buffalo were left in the wild."[20]

---

20 From "Where the Buffalo No Longer Roamed: The Transcontinental Railroad connected East and West—and accelerated the destruction of what had been in the center of North America." Gilbert King. smithsonian.com. July 17, 2012. <http://www.smithsonianmag.com/history/where-the-buffalo-no-longer-roamed-3067904/?no-ist>

Ted was a key person in the signaling division. He was based out of the same office facility as me, but he was often on the road seeing to equipment and training. It was why he knew the comings and goings of Cardew Station so well.

From the office, signalmen along the line or yard masters were telegraphed, directing them to set stop signals for trains or send them onto sidings as other trains passed. It was a coordinated dance which depended on knowing all of the routes, being able to make calculations about speed, understanding priorities, and then developing a plan to direct the movements of the trains. The system was all about motion and communication.

Throughout my morning I thought about the explosion.

When I saw Ted, at lunch, I asked him when it was decided that our train back would stop at the unused station.

"Maybe ten days ago," he said.

"Were other passengers aware of the stop?"

"No, it was only for Miss Wyndham."

"Do you know how many people would have known about the train stopping there, and what time it was going to be sitting in the station?"

"It's impossible to say, but probably not many. Signaling people of course." He looked at me curiously. "Why?"

"Just wondering."

"No, I think you have a reason. Are you thinking that the bomb was set to go off when the train was in the station?"

"I have been wondering about that, yes."

"It sounds like you think it was set by a railroad person."

"Don't you? No one should have gotten off besides us. Think about it. Isn't that significant? I assume that the guy who warned us got off the train. I didn't see him on the platform when we pulled into the station. Only a few people knew the train was stopping there and they would have been railroad employees, therefore the guy who got off and knew of the explosion must have been a railroad employee."

I went on, "The cops are apparently saying they think a railroad union was responsible. I was dismissive of the idea at first but now I'm thinking that it's possible since it looks like a railroad man was involved. What made the idea of union involvement at first seem dubious to me was that blowing up a little shack accomplishes nothing. So now I'm thinking that maybe the idea was to bomb the train. Just lucky that it had already left the station. It didn't say so in the paper, but I suspect it's what the cops are thinking. Trains are at the heart of America. Blowing one up is big symbolic news!"

"If that's what they think, they're all wet. Even if the train was right beside the station that little bomb wouldn't have done much damage to it. It's not the way to blow up a train. And why would a union bomb a train full of railroad people? It makes no sense."

"Okay then" I hesitated in thought, "so maybe they didn't want to destroy the train. Maybe they just wanted to scare the company or frighten people away from riding the train. Maybe the small bomb means that they weren't out to hurt anyone, because thinking about it, that guy at the station who was involved did warn us to keep away."

Ted didn't reply, which I took to be a concession that what I'd conjectured made sense.

Later that day the police visited Ted and asked him the same questions I had. When was the decision made to have the train stop at the small station and who might've known about it?

Ted told me afterward that he'd volunteered that they were on the wrong trail if they thought the train was the target of the attack from a small bomb inside the station. In response, a cop had blurted out that the bomb wasn't in the station house. It had been attached to the outside of it, at the top of the steps to the parking lot. The inference being that the intention was to hurt exiting passengers.

He added that they were also considering that the bomb might well be the start of a wave of terror against the railroad, so extra security had been laid on at every railroad station, especially downtown at Briggs Terminal.[21]

After Ted relayed the details of his conversation with the police I lost all confidence in my conjecture that the bombing had been a symbolic gesture. It now sounded like the police did indeed have some evidence that they weren't disclosing and the evidence said that the bombing was a murder attempt.

---

21 In passing, it can be noted that Briggs Terminal (like many other notable and beautiful stations) was torn down (in 1961). A few years later and it would have been saved. The tearing down of Penn Station in New York City prompted an outrage which led to heritage building preservation laws in NYC and nationally. Older train stations like this were once significant landmarks that uniquely identified cities – like churches and government buildings had before them – their magnificence perhaps being symbolically significant. Stations were the hub of cities and towns organized around train transportation and commerce. Now, of course, most major station design is simply functional, and perhaps tall buildings and skylines have become more important to cities' identities. The huge downtown communications towers in many places, in particular, brag of global connectedness as they literally break free from the constraints of the city.

The newspaper story didn't include the names of any of the four people who'd come close to being blown up. It only said that, "two recently returned soldiers and their companions who departed at the stop had just made it away from the station when the explosion occurred." Not quite the whole story.

No mention that one of the "companions" was Charlotte Wyndham (which would have sold millions of newspapers across the country), and no mention that the other was Maxine Spires (whose presence might give the investigation higher priority).

I wondered if the police had withheld their names because one of them was the wife of K&L's owner. Maybe Maxine had requested it to keep her affair with Ted a secret from

John. Her husband was the wealthiest man in the area, and politically well connected, so I think the cops would have obliged if she did.

It struck me that if the press knew that Maxine was near the bombing it would have undoubtedly sent eager reporters looking for quotes from the Spires family, and had them developing conspiracy theories that the bomb was meant for Maxine as union retaliation against Mr. Spires.

Maybe it was the police who kept her name under wraps to keep their investigation secret.

Since I believed that a railroad man was behind the bombing, it followed that the likely target was Maxine. It all came back to the unions. What better way to punish John Spires than to kill his wife and simultaneously get it in the news that she was with a man who was not her husband? There was nothing wrong with her being with Ted, as far as that went, but yellow journalism being what it is I think it would have been made into a big deal.

There was an obvious problem with the union retribution theory though. The only reason we weren't killed was because of a tip by the man singing *Casey Jones*. He saved us from getting hurt, which he wouldn't have done if that was the plan.

But then again, I thought, it was still plausible that the original plan had indeed been to hurt Maxine but it had been aborted at the last minute. Perhaps because the bomber discovered that Charlotte Wyndham was with us. Seeing her could have come as a shock. Killing someone not connected to the railroad, especially a national icon who supported working people, wouldn't be something the unions would want.

It was a highly speculative theory but I arrived home

thinking it to be persuasive. After all – the newspaper story said the bomb was on a timer – so there was no reason for a bomber to get off the train and risk his own life. He would have only done it for a reason, and what better reason than to save a famous writer and a couple of railroad people. The day before I had come to the aid of a union man. The wife of the railroad owner might have been fair game, but not me, Ted, or Charlotte.

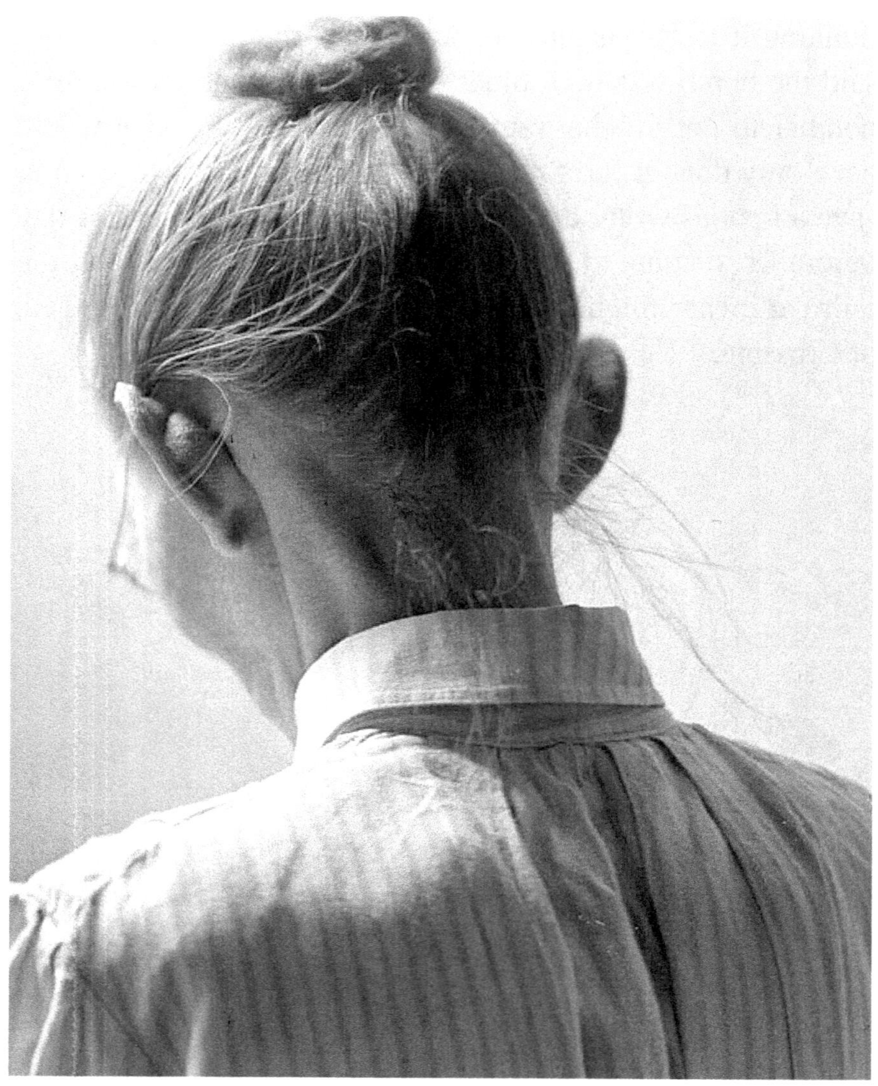

In my mailbox on Tuesday was a short note from Charlotte Wyndham inviting me round to her place the next evening; right after dinner. She explained that she was sending the note because she didn't have a phone in her cabin. I'd read once, somewhere, that she lived in some sort of Utopian farming community she'd founded out in the bush.

Enclosed were directions from Cardew Station.

I arrived around seven p.m., but being September it was still bright and sunny. I had my taxi drop me at a gate across the drive.

A hand-painted sign on a post read, "We have no interest in selling this property."

I climbed the gate and walked up the narrow dirt drive which ran among dense forest, and noted that this had never been a farm. I passed an old, but well kept up house, which had presumably belonged to an earlier owner of the land. It wasn't far beyond the house, maybe a hundred feet, where the road swung to the right, and immediately on rounding the curve I had my first glimpse of several cabins. I knew that Charlotte's place was the last on the right.

I found her working in a huge garden beside it.

She stood up and waved when she saw me, and made her way to the road where I greeted her.

"Let's walk," she said immediately. "I want to take you back to Evelyn's."

We went slowly, with Charlotte pointing things out along the way.

I commented on the beauty of the place. There was a valley off to the right and some of the cabins had incredible vistas.

"It's completely isolated from the city but near enough that the women who live here can easily get downtown," Charlotte said. "The closest bus stop is only a ten minute walk. Evelyn, for one, likes to go into town. She'd go more often but I keep her pretty busy. Right now she's part of a group pushing President Truman's idea for national public health insurance and, as always, she volunteers at a local hospital."

I now understood the sign at the gate. Hopeful buyers were undoubtedly around regularly to ask if Charlotte was willing to sell so they could develop the property. It was the direction things were going. The government was going all out building roads to cater to the automobile which meant that people could travel further to work. With a car, people are free to live wherever they choose, but it was leading to the destruction of natural areas like this one.

I wasn't opposed to cars, but I preferred trains. They let people be passive, look about and interact with each other. Cars, on the other hand, keep you isolated, demand your attention and that you always be occupied.[22]

I imagined real estate moguls salivating at the thought of turning this beautiful expanse into streets, shops and exclusive homes. The area of expensive homes that had taken over Cardew ended just before Charlotte's property and beyond that were cliffs looking out over a large lake. This was the very definition of scarce, prime real estate.

---

22 It may be noted (while I generally try to avoid connecting observations with modern views) that this rudimentary sort of observation about cars has been developed by many analysts since. Jacques Ellul and Michel Foucault, for example, talked about the anonymity of maneuvering a hunk of steel through an artificial environment as a loss of subjectivity.

"How much land do you have here?" I asked.

"Six-hundred acres. It was inexpensive at the time that I bought it but I wanted to get a big enough tract so that if the city expanded – like it's doing now – that we'd remain surrounded by forest."

"I understand this is a Utopian society for women."

"No, no. Some journalist put that in a story somewhere and it stuck. But it's not. I have no religious-like desires to build an Eden or operate a nunnery, so I've no wish to tell others how to live within a predetermined plan sent down from on high, especially not women who have fought against the rules made for them by society or husbands. What we have here is a community of women writers looking for solitude to work and a supportive environment to do so. It's not a writers' colony where temporary residents are subsidized. Here, women can stay as long as they wish. It's a community where women have homes. My inheritance covers the taxes and electricity, but other than that people pay for their own stuff. Whatever else they have is their business. I have no phone, or electricity or running water in my cabin, but the other women do. Otherwise, it's somewhat communal. We share a large vegetable and fruit garden, orchard, eat dinner together, and have gatherings in the evenings, although people can opt out of any of it. The big thing is to facilitate women's writing, even if the writer is dead broke."

"But they'd all have some income from writing, wouldn't they?"

"Not necessarily. Having one's writing published is not a requirement for residence."

"How long have you lived here?"

"Twenty-five years. I bought the land in 1921 and a cabin

or two is added every four or five years. Hopefully the place will continue after I die. Evelyn will get what's left of my estate after I'm gone so what happens will be up to her. Possibly she'll find a benefactress."

Editor's note: The significance and size of the garden and orchard are not sufficiently explained here to understand if Wyndham's views drew from the ideas of Louisa Manners, niece of her dead young lover [whose views were not unlike those of certain modern anarchists who emphasize the meeting of "needs" in a direct way, with minimal commodities, enhancing self-sufficiency, although not necessarily advocating land ownership and farms].

After Manners became known for her stance against newspapers, she was criticized for "avoiding life" although she said in some of the stories about her that the turning away she advocated was in order to embrace life, her life, without being told by others what was important and what equated with "life". Her personal proscription was also to limit one's geographic horizon, the more so the better, to grow, create and live with freedom, and to be in a position to help those around us; our area of ethical responsibility.

When WW1 came a small scale method of food production – similar to what Manners advocated – was ironically employed to feed citizens during this unnecessary and bloody power struggle between imperial governments, where common people were cannon fodder, their own governments and newspaper drum-pounding being the biggest threats to their freedom.

They were called "Victory Gardens", their radical aspect being defanged by calling them part of the "war effort", where food could be produced on any patch of land by anyone, no government being needed.

Hugely successful, they mostly disappeared after the war. There was apparently no longer anything to justify such supposed "self-sacrifice". Freedom meant the freedom to buy loads of stuff produced by others.

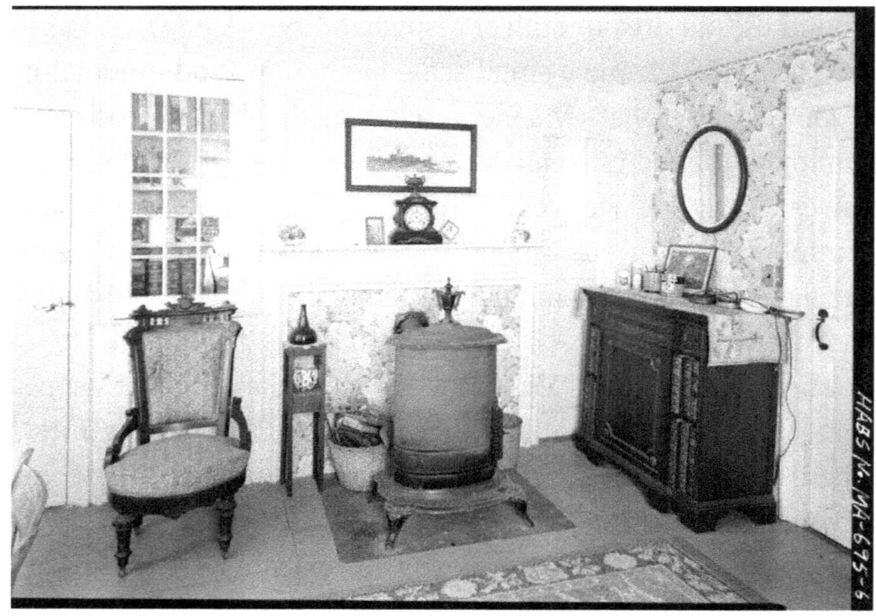

We knocked on the door of the old house close to the road. The furnishings had a quaint, warn, old-fashioned look.

The door was answered by a woman introduced as Evelyn Carter. She looked to be age fifty or so. I was told that Evelyn helped Charlotte with her affairs. That's how she was introduced, not as an assistant or employee, but as a friend who helped.

"I dictate my books to Evelyn," said Charlotte, nodding towards a crowded desk in the corner with a typewriter on it. (I learned later that Charlotte paid Evelyn for this work.)

"So you would be a writer too," I said to Evelyn, "since you live here." I hadn't recognized her name.

"Yes," she answered. "Just one novel in 1922 when I was in my twenties. You won't have heard of me. No one here is famous like Charlotte but especially not me. I'm at work on my second novel however and I expect that its publication will generate nary a small ripple of notice."

"Oh, are you almost done?" I asked enthusiastically. "I'll read it."

"I don't think I'm that close to the end and I don't know when I'll finish it. I've been working on it since I finished the last one."

I must have looked surprised.

Charlotte laughed and smiled at me. "Yes, that's 24 years. It's the Herculean aesthetic that I expect will become popular now that Mr. Joyce's last book, which came out at the start of the war – so was seventeen years in the making – is now being called a work of genius."

"My book is changing," said Evelyn. "Since the war, with the dead and the injured, and the growth of tyranny, literature can't be preoccupied with experimentation. There's too much at stake."

Charlotte – known for her literary experimentation – said nothing. I wondered for a second if Evelyn's remark signaled some friction between the women.

After tea had been made and served, Charlotte turned to me.

"I'm glad you're here. As I told Evelyn, I enjoyed our talk the other day and hope we shall be friends. I planned to invite you here at some point but I asked you to come today because there's something I want to talk to you about."

I set down my cup and gave her my attention.

"I have been given to understand," she said, "that the police think that one of the railroad unions was involved in the bombing at Cardew Station. Or at least that's what was apparently said on the radio. Do you know if they have any proof for that being the case, or is it just speculation? They haven't been here to see me."

"I can't say whether they have anything, as they haven't paid me a follow up visit either. It could just be anti-union speculation but maybe the police have some evidence."

"And what about you? Do you have a theory?"

"Well, I'm a little hesitant to say but I do think that the bombing was done by a railroad man. The Cardew stop is unused. It was Ted who arranged for the train to stop there so no one knew about it except a few railroad people. The bomb was timed to go off at the same time the train was there so the bomber knew the train would stop. It points to the unions or at least someone associated with the railroad."

Charlotte looked thoughtful, considering my comment.

"So you think the bomb was intended to blow up the train?" Charlotte said.

"No. At first I thought so but Ted tells me the bomb was too small plus there's no way the unions would blow up a train filled with railroad people. It seems to me – and Ted said it was his impression that it's what the police think too – that the bombing was a murder attempt since the bomb was placed by the stairs. My theory is that a person was being targeted and that would've been Maxine Spires, to punish the railroad's owner, since everything suggests union people were involved."

"But what about that obscure warning you picked up on? It doesn't sound like the bomber wanted to hurt anyone."

"Perhaps, but it makes me think they called off the plan when they realized it wasn't just Maxine and some man getting off. So the bomber warned us in a way that allowed him to get away before I realized what I'd been told." I'm sure I looked pleased with myself.

"That makes no sense though," said Charlotte. "There's no reason railroad people would have known Maxine was going to get off there, little own with a man. When we were on the train she told me herself that she'd only decided to come that morning. Plus, why would union people go after Maxine and not her husband? It's a pretty round about way of attacking him.

"It's funny though," she continued, "I think you and I are on similar tracks, only my conclusions are the exact opposite. If the bomber was targeting someone I suspect it was me. It was the rest of you being there that they wouldn't have expected. Remember, I was the only one meant to get off at Cardew Station, and I was the reason the train stopped. It was supposed to be just me on the platform, and I suppose Evelyn, who was to meet me there … although she was a little bit late. In any case, none of you three were expected to be there."

That definitely put a different slant on things. "But who'd want to kill you?" It seemed a dubious idea.

"Very many people. If you want to see threatening letters, Evelyn here will show them to you."

Evelyn pointed to the desk.

"But who knew you'd be on the train?"

"Lots of people I suspect, but I don't know for sure. When I was invited to come and receive a check, the railroad foundation's letter said that the train would stop to pick me up at Cardew Station and drop me off there. So it could have been mentioned around by someone at Maxine's foundation."

"Do you know that for certain?"

"No, I don't. You'd have to ask Maxine who she told. Or

her daughter more like it. She's the one we corresponded with. Maxine runs the foundation but I think it's Victoria who does the work and calls the shots.[23] You know, I wonder if instead of just trying to figure out who was being targeted, that the police might spend some time considering who it was that the man giving us the warning was trying to save. That could point to who the target was. And they should also ask whether it even was a warning. The singing fella might have simply been gloating that we were about to die and not trying to save anyone at all."

____

23 The largess of this company does not mean that their motive for existing wasn't profit but community and altruism, as John Spires often stated. Of course, like other corporations and large businesses it was selfish and profit driven. Huge tax breaks are publicly justified by pointing to a company's charitable donations (although they're invariably a pittance compared to the amount of their tax break). Although well-intentioned by Victoria Spires, no doubt, the company, through its foundation, just shared a bit of the money not spent on taxes as a marketing ploy to justify not paying taxes and to mask its true nature. This is also the means by which the aims and priorities of social welfare spending are decided by the wealthy rather than by elected governments.

Victoria rang me the next evening, Thursday, at the agreed upon time. We were going to discuss the upcoming weekend. I think she'd arranged to be alone when she called. I gathered she was sitting in her father's study with the door closed. He was still out of town.

I was extremely pleased to hear her voice.

She went right to the explosion. "It makes me sick thinking what could've happened," she said.

I asked about her mother.

"Oh, she's resilient. I'm more in shock than she is. My father phoned us after the police spoke to him and he's outraged, not surprisingly. ... Thank God for the warning you got. I don't suppose you've seen Charlotte Wyndham or know how she's doing?"

"As a matter of fact I saw her last night. She's unshakable.

She invited me over to ask if I knew whether unions were behind the bombing. Or, I guess it was more to ask if I knew if the police had any evidence for what's being said in the papers about the unions being behind the bombing. Charlotte thinks the bomb was intended for her since she was the only one scheduled to get off at Cardew and that the bomber was likely someone upset by her writing. If we were warned at the last minute about the danger – and she's not convinced we were – it might've been because she turned out to have company. Even if she's right, it doesn't help us get to the bomber though, since she said there could've been a bunch of people who were aware of the plan to drop her off at Cardew Station."

I asked Victoria if she knew how many people would've known about that.

"I can't say. Not many. My mother told me to ask Ted to set up the unscheduled stop for Charlotte, and she didn't mention anyone else. And Ted was the only one I spoke to. There could be something in what Charlotte's saying though, about it being widely known that she would depart at Cardew. One of the trains stopped to pick her up on Saturday, remember. There were a lot of railroad people aboard, coming here for the ceremony, who would've seen. It wouldn't take much of a guess to deduce that she'd be dropped off there on the trip home."

"That makes sense. What seems to me unlikely though is that a train person, or anyone for that matter, would want to kill an old lady. I know her books are controversial and she gets hate mail, but to kill someone for them?"

"Yes," Victoria thought about it a moment, "but if the bomb was meant for her it could've been prompted by something other than her books."

"Something else? Like what?"

"Well, I've followed her career since I was a young teen and she was involved in some pretty radical stuff in her younger days."

I thought about my sister's love of Charlotte's novels. They obviously appealed to young women. "What sort of stuff?"

"Charlotte was one of the suffragettes who worked with Alice Paul's group; the radical faction of the suffrage movement. She was a member of the Silent Sentinels, the group who paraded outside the White House six days a week to humiliate the President. They were a brave lot who got beaten up by the police and by passing men. In jail, they went on hunger strikes and were force fed with tubes down their throats. They were beaten and tortured but it didn't stop them."

"Did they hurt anyone; the suffragettes I mean?"

"Not in general. They were non-violent, practicing civil disobedience. They were only interested in the publicity.

They staged parades, for example. Women would dress up with gowns, representations of freedom, or hope, or other concepts. Inez Boissevain, who was a lawyer, led one suffrage parade wearing a white cape while riding a horse in Washington, D.C.. You know those pictures I showed you where I dress up? I didn't say so but part of our reason for doing them is to copy those women. That's why some of our costumes are white robes, which was the suffragette color. The racy pictures are our own bit of radicalism in that spirit although it's only men who see them as sexual rather than as being about celebrating women, our history, our nature, and our inter-relationships."

"So they didn't hurt anyone then. They didn't bomb people."

"I didn't say that. Strictly speaking, they were trying to be outrageous so who knows what else they got up to … But that makes me think. Charlotte began as a suffragette in England and only moved here in 1916 when Alice Paul began the National Woman's Party. British suffragettes were definitely destructive. They used bombs, burned rail cars and empty railroad stations, destroyed art and attacked cultural centers like the National Gallery, Westminster Abbey, the British Museum, plus lots of politicians. They were physically violent and fought back against male dominance and culture. Many learned jujitsu. One woman even horse-whipped Winston Churchill. And they did those things despite the fact that the cops were even more brutal to them than here. I don't know what Charlotte got up to over there, if anything. Maybe it's why she came to America."

"So she might have blown up empty train buildings in England," I said, pondering. "Geez, I wonder if she thought the Cardew bomb was retribution for something, or maybe even a message."

"Who knows, but it wouldn't surprise me. It would explain the strange nature of the murder attempt. There are lots of easier ways to kill someone. Plus don't forget, Charlotte also lives near the station and could have local enemies. Heck, she used to travel on the suffrage tours and speak to groups. They'd travel about on the train and stop at various stations. Something might have happened at Cardew Station."

A local connection? I thought about the land Charlotte owned and the amount of money that could be made if she was out of the way and it was obtained by a developer. A theory with zero evidence to back it up, but not something to dismiss out of hand.

And another possibility soon followed. Hearing how Charlotte had once been a suffragette and that they'd bombed railway stations, the thought crossed my mind – to then be immediately dismissed as ludicrous – that Charlotte herself could've been involved in the bombing. I said nothing of either idea.

We continued our conversation and talked about the coming Saturday afternoon. There were three trains running on Saturday and we decided I'd board the one leaving at noon so would arrive at Victoria's house around two p.m.. I'd return home after dinner. It was a two hour trip each way but I could use the time to catch up on some work.

I was pleased with the prospect of seeing Victoria but felt fairly certain her father wouldn't be too thrilled to see me, even though my get-together with Victoria was just an afternoon's visit to go for a walk, quite innocent on the face of it.

It wasn't that her father didn't like me – we'd met a number of times through work and he was always very friendly in that context – but Victoria was a twenty-year-old socialite and I was his twenty-six-year-old employee with no guarantee of ever rising in the company or of ever having much of an income. If I was someone like her father, firmly rooted in upper class society, or trying to be, I wouldn't have liked me as a potential suitor either.

I wouldn't have said so to Victoria, but I thought that Maxine's reaction was even more likely to be negative than her father's. After all, I knew about Maxine's affair with Ted, and the prospect of me having a close personal relationship with her daughter, the kind where you share everything, might be extremely worrisome for her.

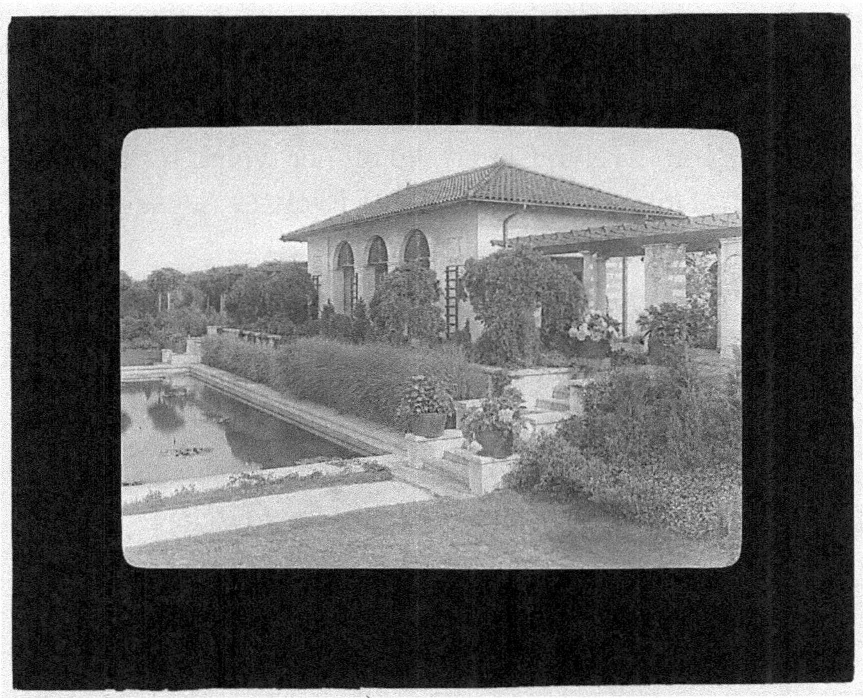

Victoria and I met at the appointed time at her house and immediately left on our walk around the grounds and down to a stream that ran behind them. It was a most enjoyable outing. I avoided questioning her about what her mother had said when told of my visit.

At one point, Victoria asked what I thought of Charlotte's "writers colony". She'd never been there but obviously wanted to.

I told her how beautiful the place was, and explained how it operated.

"What did you think of that arrangement?"

"It's admirable. Self-sacrificing."

"Yes. It's pretty Spartan though and isolated. It obviously works for those women. It sounds appealing to me. I'd love to live there sometime. Did Charlotte say whether she was doing any writing?"

"No, and it's hard to tell if she is or isn't. She mentioned that her friend, Evelyn Carter, did all her typing for her and I saw a lot of papers on the desk at Evelyn's house but they could've been Evelyn's own book."

After about two hours of walking and talking, Victoria expressed an interest in going home since her father was due to arrive shortly.

I quietly took a deep breath. Seeing her parents was the part of my visit that I wasn't looking forward to.

As we approached a garden wall we could hear voices.

Victoria smiled and strode forward, ahead of me, but she stopped before stepping around the hedge where the speakers were.

When I caught up and stood beside her I recognized the voices as those of her parents.

Victoria was listening and no longer smiling.

"Then why'd you get off at that little station?" I heard John Spires ask, in an obviously angry voice.

"Why not?" Maxine was far more controlled.

"Because it's ten miles from the downtown station and your hotel."

"We got off to see the old lady home. You know that."

"I know no such thing. There was no reason for you to do

that. Those men with you live near there, I can understand if they decided at the last minute to get off, but not you, you were going to a hotel across the road from the next station. Plus that "old lady" as you call her needed no help. She got to the station without any help from us and she certainly could've gotten home without it."

"So what are you saying?"

"That you got off because you weren't going to the hotel. You got off because you were going to spend the night at the home of your lover."

"Whew!"

"Everyone knows about it. You think I'm blind? Did you think by not telling me you were going to the city while I was away on my business trip that I wouldn't find out about it? What did you say to your daughter beforehand, 'I'm going shopping in the city but don't tell your father so he won't chide me for spending too much money', or something along those lines? As if I don't know about the way you carry on."

"Your suspicions are crazy. I was helping that poor old lady …"

"'Poor' she isn't. That old lady's sitting on a goldmine. She doesn't understand that land is real estate and not some Utopia. I played along about the company foundation helping her, but I still don't know why you wanted to give her money to give to some kids when she has lots of it of her own."

"… and I stayed at the hotel," Maxine said with finality.

"So where's the receipt?"

"I didn't keep it."

"I can check with the hotel."

"Do it."

"And that'll give me evidence in a divorce trial. Not as good as you getting exposed in the newspapers for being at Cardew Station with your lover would've been – so the world could see what you're like – but it'll do. Ah, what a shame the names of the four people at the bombing didn't get into the papers. I could have used some sympathy after the strike."

"You sound like you're the one who set off the bomb, to get your accusations aired in the newspapers."

"Ha! If I wanted to expose anything all I'd have to do

would be to hire a detective and reveal the evidence in court."

"And just to clarify; it was your daughter who decided to give that woman some money, not me. I didn't even know who she was."

Victoria stood silently after the conversation stopped. One of the parties, I gathered, had stalked off.

Victoria turned and walked towards the side door of the house.

I followed.

When we got to the door, she stopped and turned. "You must've known about this," she said. "If what my father says is true, you would've known. Ted's your best friend. So is it true?"

"I didn't think it was my business to say anything. I didn't want to come between you and your mother."

"You better go now. I'll be okay tomorrow, but you better go. I don't want to be around anyone."

On the long milk run ride back home, stopping at station after station, I considered whether I should have said anything to Victoria about her mother. I felt bad for her. She'd not only seen an ugly incident involving her parents but had heard her father speaking of divorce.

I decided that I'd give Victoria a few days to let these things settle and phone her in the coming week.

On the train I weighed the idea that Victoria's father was responsible for the bombing and that he did it to expose his wife's affair and gain him sympathy.

It seemed to me to be highly unlikely. As Spires said, if it was publicity he was after he could've gotten a detective to get proof of Maxine's infidelity and then had a big splashy divorce trial – that is, if he even knew about the infidelity which I wasn't convinced was the case. And if he didn't know about it then he definitely wouldn't have set a bomb.

Maxine's presence had actually been kept out of the press, suggesting that John had used his influence with the police to keep it a secret. It refuted the idea that he was out to expose her. Realistically, he, like many people, wouldn't want his personal business splashed all over the news.

On top of those objections was the fact that no one knew that anyone other than Charlotte Wyndham would be getting off the train at Cardew.

I was still of a mind to think that whoever set the bomb either intended to kill Charlotte or just to give the appearance of it. Perhaps the person who got off the train when we did – the one who tipped us off about the bomb – did so specifically to make sure that she didn't get hurt.

But why would anyone want to get it into the newspapers that there had been a failed attempt on the life of the famous writer? That made no sense.

Charlotte was right, there was no way Maxine was the target of the bomber.

Since I was now convinced that the bombing had nothing to do with Maxine I was back to my original way of thinking, that a railroad union had planted the bomb for some purpose; to retaliate against the railroad or perhaps to scare people away from using the train. The bomb could have been meant to create the illusion that it was intended either to blow up the train or to kill someone.

I'd dismissed out of hand Charlotte's thought that we hadn't been warned. A man had followed us then whispered into my ear and run away in full view when he could've stayed on the train and done nothing. So no, we were warned.

I turned to my newspaper that I'd picked up before boarding my train. "Union Terror!" was the headline of an editorial. It argued that unions were filled with Reds seeking to disrupt the "American way of life" so the railroad unions needed to be investigated.

Something in it made me think of the Mukden Incident in 1931 where the Japanese planted a small amount of explosives by a railroad line. The track wasn't destroyed and trains kept passing over it, but it was the staged pretext for Japan to blame Chinese dissidents, and thus to justify their invasion and occupation of Manchuria.[24] In a similar way, the Cardew explosion was being used as a way to undermine the union movement with no proof required.[25]

Could John Spires have staged this explosion to make it appear that the unions were out of control and to turn public opinion against them? It was possible. It was like the rationale of the suffragettes in blowing up empty buildings.

If the intention of the bomber had only been publicity, it would account for the bomber's warning. I couldn't see anyone in the railroad union wanting to kill Charlotte Wyndham. She was a national icon and sympathetic with working people. But would someone working for John Spires have the same kind of scruples? Maybe Charlotte Wyndham was meant to die. It would have gotten world-wide attention. It might have been Maxine getting off the train that saved Charlotte's life by mandating a change of plan.

I was suddenly appalled at my own cynicism. And I instantly wondered how I could ever tell Victoria about my suspicions regarding her father.

____

24 Perhaps this is in the nature of all real and fake terrorism. Even so-called anarchist terrorism is an attempt to be part of the political spectacle.

25 Recall again that one year after the strikes of 1946 there was a legal attack on unions mandating that communists were not allowed to be part of union leadership. Approval for this sort of law requires fear, and newspapers play their role in whipping up the requisite hysteria and paranoia. Here, the newspaper was linking communists (as the evil "Red Menace") to unions and damning them by association. Communists were defined as "un-American".

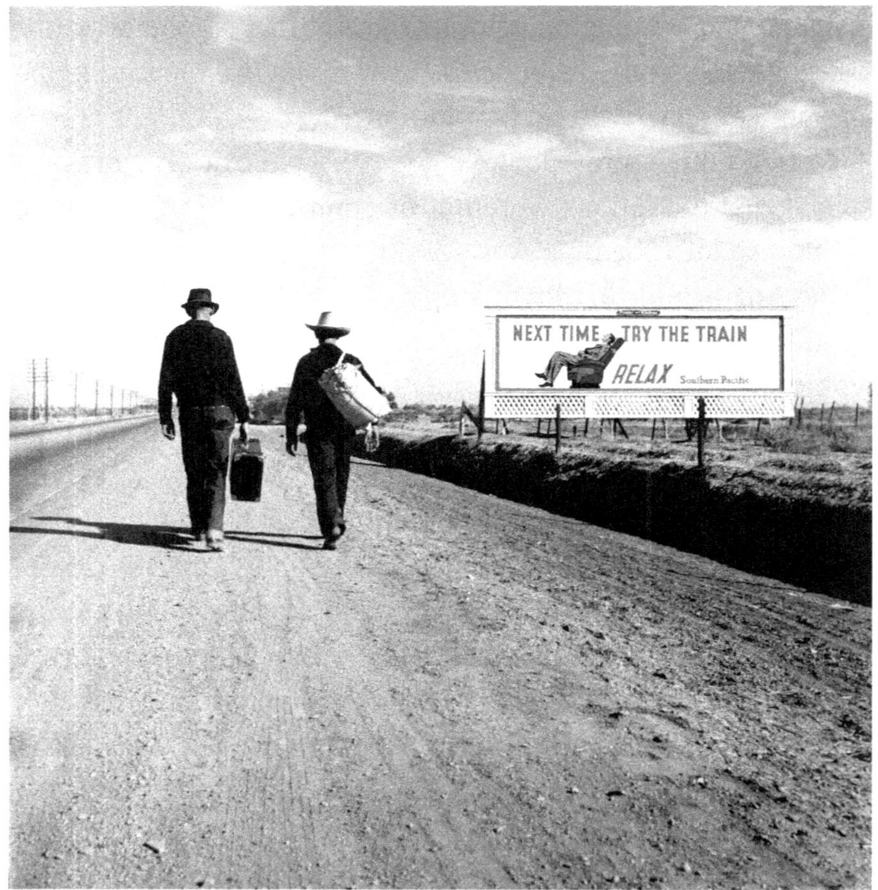

I reflected on the fact that, somehow, I'd begun to cast myself in the role of detective seeking out the bomber. (But invariably wrong in my case, my theories corrected by every person I spoke to.) Actually, I wasn't acting like a real detective. The real ones were probably out tracking down the mystery man who'd gotten off the train, advancing based on concrete evidence, interviewing passengers and people in the area who may have seen him. All I was doing was trying to understand a plausible reason for the bombing.

I thought of Agatha Christie's Poirot. He used psychology

to ferret out the villain. It was an approach for the pre-war age that reflected the new fascination with psychology, popularizing it. The detective devised a theory, a pseudo-scientific approach, so the modern reader would be impressed. We trust people who devise theories.[26]

I wondered what there was from the post-war period that I could draw on. Atomic weapons were new of course, but that wouldn't help me here. Engineering perhaps, and our love of new technology. Or something new, like more and more cars on more and more highways. Or the growth of television; increasing numbers of people sitting nightly in their own homes, absorbed with these shadow images of reality, like prisoners in Plato's cave.

And then, as my train crossed over a highway, I noticed through the window, a wall of advertising billboards. There were so many that the natural world behind them was blocked from drivers' views. What drivers would now see was the gleaming new world depicted in the signs. A Xanadu for sale,

---

26 More significant, I think, is that the spy and the fictional detective provide people with the comforting notion that in a sinister world filled with enemies, where we are faced with the ontological fact that we can only know our own thoughts (or even confirm our own existence) that we can discern the innermost thoughts of others. They fulfill a hope for people who almost only ever meet with strangers – those whose outer appearance can belie a twisted inner reality – that the danger of this can be overcome, and that we live in a sane, just, and objective world. In Conway's further comments we can also see the man of science's assurance in an objective reality of facts slipping away. Metaphysics died with the atomic bomb. Psychology is a rear-guard action based on the assumption that people's subjective states reveal a shared reality.

told through pictures where nothing was real.

I thought about my ruminations on illusion. I didn't know what was real or what was staged with regards to the bombing at Cardew Station. Was the bombing like an advertisement, meant to sell us something? Was everything about it fake, like one of Victoria's photos?[27] (Although this struck me as an apt characterization of all photos. They are supposedly worth a thousand words about something, but a photo is like a single jig-saw piece, no longer part of a larger unified world, so it is ambiguous.[28] We think we understand them but we don't.[29])

---

27 Obviously the proliferation of images and their supplanting of reality has been a major subject of analysis for a long time so I don't take it up here. (Some even argue that images are concepts. Some of Victoria's were that, of course.)

28 One could argue that this freezing of life was critical in bringing about modernity. Photography disembodies the day-to-day so it is no longer a continuous experience, self-mediated, involving all of the senses, but that it is now outwardly mediated and open to the gaze. E.g. Barbara Duden, in *Disembodying Women: Perspectives on Pregnancy and the Unborn* (Cambridge: Harvard University Press, 1993), argues that the technical ability to make a woman's interior subject to the gaze (through ultrasound, x-ray, intra-uterine photography etc.) was significant in the remaking of women's bodies into systems managed by experts.

29 In "On Photography," Susan Sontag said photos provide "evidence" (but notes that what gets shown and how it is shown can be done in ways to manipulate us). I would argue (as others have) that all photos are lies.

Uncertainty also applied to every individual involved in the Cardew bombing. Charlotte was not who she seemed to be to the public; the demure Victorian. Maxine was all pretense, exuding class and marital happiness. Victoria was not the straight laced daughter. None matched their photographic record or appearance.

In that vein, all of us were making assumptions about what was real or not with respect to the explosion; including the police and me, the fake detective.

I went back over what I did feel some certainty about.

1. The train had been scheduled to stop at Cardew so Charlotte could get off.

2. The decision for the rest of us to get off there was made at the last moment.

3 ... I hesitated.

Was the decision a last minute one? It was made by Ted. When had he made it? Who had he told about it? This mattered because, if the bomb had been intended to kill Charlotte and the warning we'd received had been because the presence of others on the platform was unexpected, then the change in plan needed to have been made while the train was on route.

Since not many people would have known about the new plan, it might point us to who the man was who was singing *Casey Jones*.

If, on the other hand, the decision for Ted and others to get off at Cardew had been made before we left, then no warning would have been necessary. The bomb could have been made inactive if Ted and friends weren't meant to die.

That would suggest that the plan, from the beginning, had been to have a bomb explode but for no one get hurt. People – especially Charlotte Wyndham – almost getting hurt would have been enough to create some big anti-union newspaper headlines.

I had that feeling you get when you are on a train in a station and you pass another train going in the opposite direction. Are they moving, or are you, or are both of you? Are you going forward and they going backward or vice versa? It's dizzying.

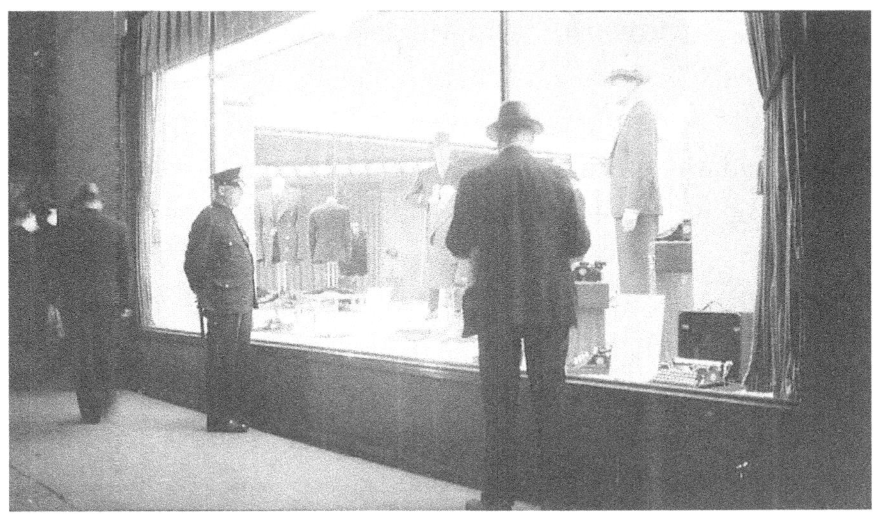

When I got home I walked the short distance to Ted's place, and found him in.

After the obligatory small talk I asked if he had heard from Maxine the previous evening.

"No. Why?"

"I had an interesting afternoon. I took the train to visit Victoria Spires." I resisted the impulse to explain why and Ted only looked blankly back at me. "We went for a walk and when we got back we heard voices arguing in the back yard. Mr. Spires had just gotten back in town and he was confronting Maxine. Victoria and I stopped where we were out of sight and listened. John was ranting and accusing Maxine of carrying on with you. She was denying it of course. John said he's known about the two of you for a long time but I think it may have only dawned on him when the cops told him after the explosion that she'd gotten off the train at Cardew Station. He could've been suspicious and checked out where we live because he said she obviously got off at Cardew intending to spend the night here with you."

"Shit," Ted frowned. "Did Maxine tell him we only got off there to see Charlotte Wyndham home?"

"Yes, but John wasn't buying it. He said that Charlotte didn't need any more help than you or I could have given her, and maybe not even that since she was going to be met at the station."

"But she was by herself …" Ted paused and then smirked, as if he was deriving some satisfaction from the matter, a sort of childish, pleased with himself grin. Ted had never really grown up. He was thirty-three-years old but still acted like a teenager where females were conquests to brag about.

He quickly went back to frowning soon enough though. I suppose the implications began setting in because he said, "I better start looking for another job I guess."

I didn't know how to respond to that but it sounded reasonable.

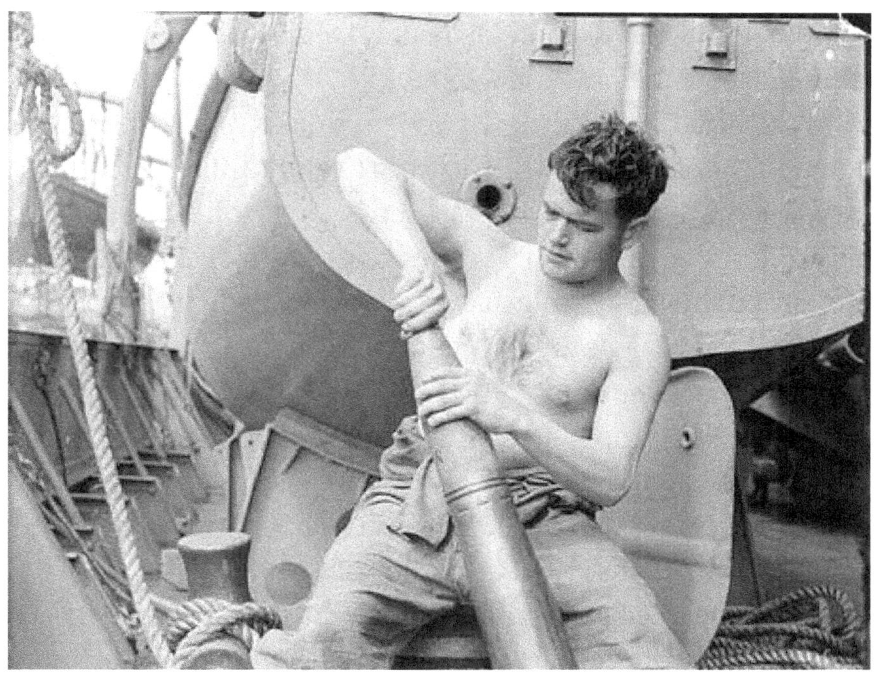

"Had any more contact with the police?" I asked Ted.

"No. You?"

"No. Oh, but I did speak to Charlotte Wyndham. She wanted to know what was happening; whether the police had any proof that one of the unions was involved. I told her what you said about the bomb not being large enough to have been intended for the train. She'd figured that out herself. She thinks, because the bomb was planted by the wooden steps, that it was intended for a person, and she figures that person was her. She thinks the bomber must have changed their mind when they saw Maxine and us. Or maybe the murderer was gloating."

"But why go after Charlotte?"

"Some people think she's a traitor."

"But even if someone wanted to kill her, planting a bomb,

coordinated with a train arrival and all that, is way too complicated a method don't you think?"

"That's true," I conceded. "So I'm thinking that maybe the bomb was only for show. If it wasn't set by some union guys to warn Spires, maybe it was set by someone meaning to blame it on the unions. The thing has been blown way out of proportion by the media and there seems to be almost no investigation. I know that no one has spoken to me or Charlotte since the day of the bombing."

Ted thought about it. I'd avoided suggesting that Spires might have had the bomb set, partly because Ted came from a union family; his father and brothers as far as I understood were in railroad unions. "Perhaps."

"I also heard that Charlotte was a suffragette here and in England. Over there they used to blow up empty train stations for publicity. So, another possibility, is that the explosion was retribution for something or a sign intended for her."

"A sign of what?"

"I don't know. That 'we're after you' perhaps."

He smiled and shook his head doubtfully.

"Oh, by the way," I said. "When did you decide that we would get off at Cardew Station?"

"I guess, about a minute before I told you, about ten minutes before getting to the station. Why?"

"I just wondered who knew. If the bomber wasn't expecting anyone to get off except Charlotte, and the bomb was meant to hurt someone, it would mean that it was intended just for her."

"Well there was enough of an explosion there to kill her and whoever she was with. … I only told the engineer and conductor about the stop and neither of them got off,"

As I walked home, I thought about Charlotte and whether she was the target of the bomb. What Ted had said gave me reason to be concerned about Charlotte. If the bomb had indeed been meant to kill her, and not as part of the labor troubles, then she could still be in danger. The attempt on her life had been unsuccessful, but that didn't mean the threat was necessarily over.

I knew that Evelyn, Charlotte's confidante, had a phone, because I'd seen it, so in the morning I called her.

She was surprised to hear from me

I said, "I've been thinking of what Charlotte was saying about the bomb when I was at your house, and I'm embarrassed that this didn't occur to me until now, but if the bomb was meant for Charlotte, as she thinks it was, then she could still be in danger. I'm worried about her."

"If her suspicions are correct, then I'd agree."

"Has she told the police about what she suspects? I think that might be a good idea."

"Oh, she won't do that."

"Why not?'

"It's like she believes in fate, although she doesn't put it quite that way. She says that if someone is out to get her then they will. I suspect she doesn't want anything to do with the police either. She has had some negative experiences. Very negative. … In any case, I suspect she's wrong about someone being after her. A bomb is no way to kill a person. She's an old lady and often feels people are after her. She's gotten threatening letters but nothing I would take seriously. Just crackpot stuff. I'm sure the police will figure things out eventually. I suspect the bomb was the work of someone angry at the railroad. That's why I haven't urged Charlotte to call the police or take any special security measures."

I said, "I don't know what the connection might be, but a

bomb in an empty building reminds me of the suffragettes that Charlotte was involved in when she was young. I wonder if there's any link."

She laughed. "Of what sort?"

"I don't know, it's just this bombing seems reminiscent of the approach."

"Well, I've heard all of Charlotte's stories of her experiences in both America and the UK, numerous times. I can pretty much guarantee you there's no connection. The idea is ludicrous to put it bluntly."

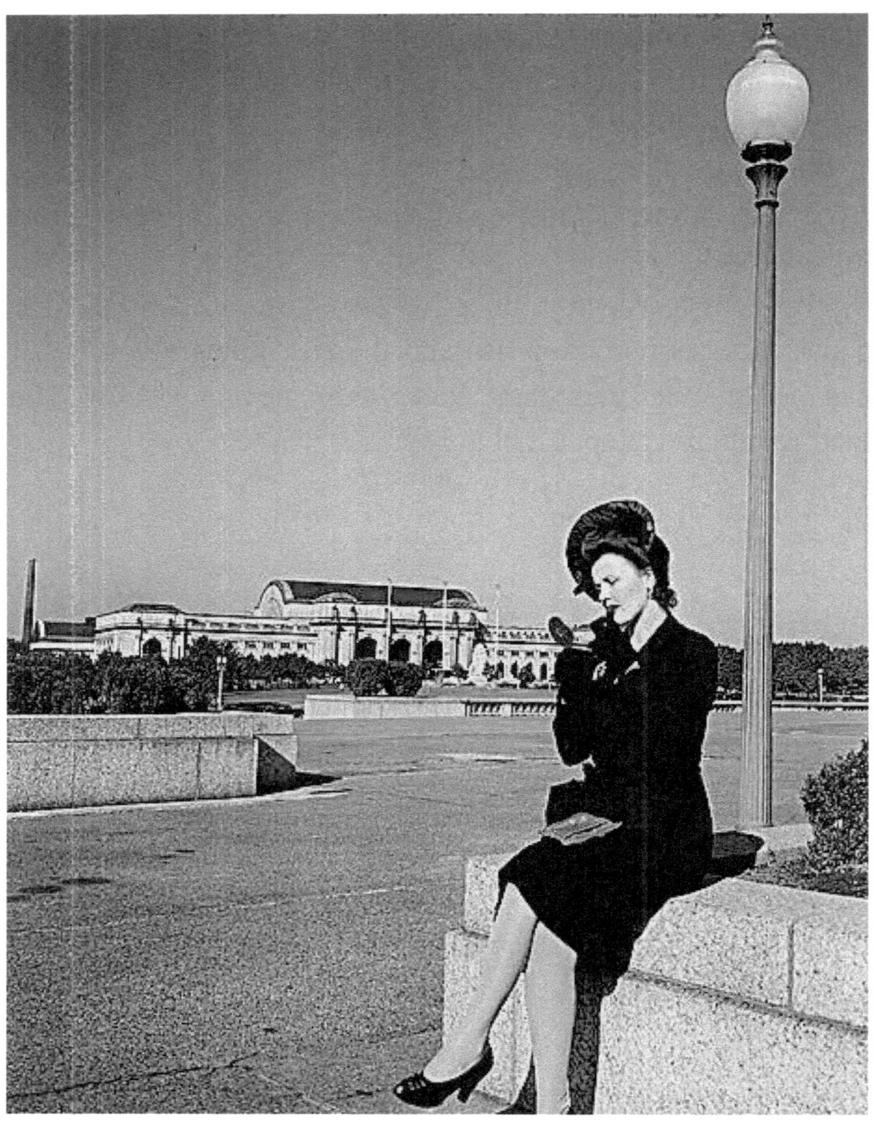

Editor's note: The subject of the drawing reproduced in the previous section, done sometime in the 1920s, is assumed to be Evelyn Carter but this is uncertain. The image above (also assumed to be of Evelyn) is from the mid 1930's and so could be more representative of how she looked in 1946. But whether this photo is actually her, however, isn't provable. It might just be an example of the street photography that was gaining in popularity at the time, expanding the gaze and the proliferation of commercial photographs.

All the people in this history are either dead or quite aged so no one can confirm that this is a photo of Evelyn. There is no other photograph to compare it to, likely because Evelyn didn't approve of "family photos" (according to one commentator), feeling they were a takeover of the aristocratic practice of hanging portraits of one's illustrious ancestors. (Perhaps the opposite conclusion regarding a lack of technique and the use of cheap technology – describing it as a way to democratize the practice of ancestor worship while knocking the artistic pretension out if it – could also have been made.)

The next day at work I asked around about the young man who had some unkind words to say about Mr. Spires at the get together the day before the bombing. It seemed everyone knew him but me.

"His name is Boyd, works in the shops, I'm surprised you don't know him."

It wasn't so surprising. I'd only been in my present position for several months, didn't share a lunchroom with the mechanical guys, and had no interaction with them.

I walked over to the shops and soon saw Boyd. He glanced in my direction as I approached but immediately looked away and continued to work in that manner which indicates a person knows you're there but doesn't want to focus on it.

"Hi Boyd," I said.

He responded in kind while continuing to look

preoccupied.

"Guess you heard about our little adventure on the train trip back from head office."

"You're a little late if you want to ask me if I set the bomb. Cops were here that same day."

"No, I know it wasn't you. The Cardew stop was planned ages before the party. The curious thing to me is that I was warned, seconds before it happened, that the bomb was about to go off. I don't know why unless someone wanted to make a big splash but with no injuries."

Boyd said nothing.

"I'm not the cops. I don't think the unions would do this. I suspect it was a sick individual – probably an employee – trying to make trouble for the railroad or the unions to turn public opinion against them. I guess … I mean, I'm hoping that if you hear anything, or suspect anyone, that you'll let me know. Not only is this person dangerous but he's got people thinking it was the unions who did it and now people are avoiding the trains which is bad for everybody."

Nothing.

I turned to walk away.

"Is it true the guy that warned you sang *Casey Jones*?" Boyd asked.

I stopped and turned back around. "Yeah."

"And that's supposed to make him a railroad person?" He laughed.

"Are there individual grudges against the railroad?"

"How long you got? There's lots. That doesn't narrow it down. I guess I owe you one though so I'll let you know if I hear anything."

Editor's note: The author once noted in an interview that he'd been to several movies over the summer of 1946. He saw three film noir flicks: *The Big Sleep* (Raymond Chandler), with its constant revelations, each one changing our perspective about the crime, *The Killers* (Hemingway), where the Swede lets himself be killed when tracked down because of something in his past, and *The Stranger*, where the noir is overtly political. Orson Welles plays a fascist who's fled to the USA and when he's discovered, he murders before he himself is killed. (In a note above it is mentioned that "Reds" were the new bête noire. Perhaps calling them the new noir would be just as accurate.)

Given the fact that there appear to be echoes of each of these movies in the author's narrative, written in the fall of that year, it gives rise to questions about its veracity; of whether it engages in the smoke and mirrors that he seems so attuned to; reality having given way to fiction.

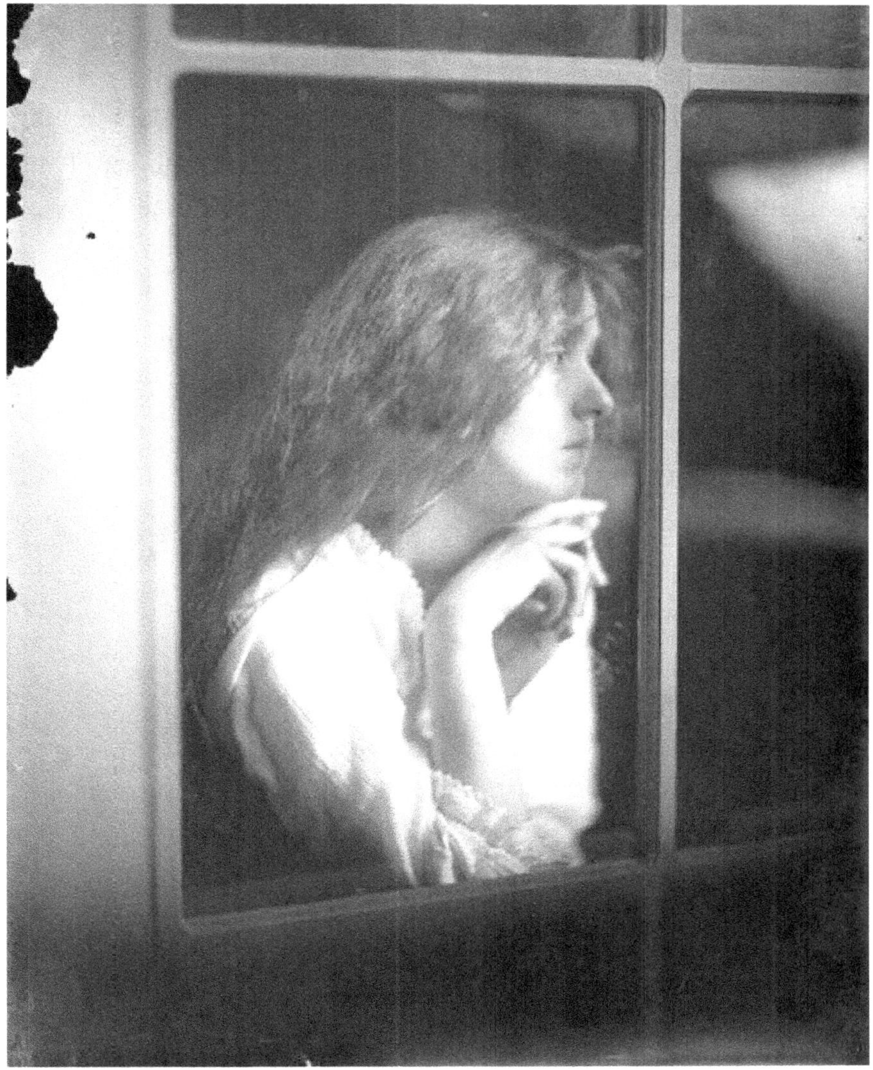

The next day Victoria called me at work and asked if she could come for a visit some time in the next few days.

"Okay. Of course," I said, surprised.

She told me that she'd been upset with me but understood why I'd said nothing about her mother's affair. She went on to say that on Saturday, after I'd left, her father opened the mail that came for him over the week he'd been away.

"He showed me a letter because I was in the study at the time. It was from the Cardew train station bomber! It had been mailed before the bombing so it was definitely from him. The writer said he'd set the bomb to publicize the way the railroad treated its union members. That it was a warning. Unless the newspaper published the included statement and the company changed its ways he would bomb again. And the next time, trains and railroad officials would be the targets."

"So it was a union thing after all."

"The man didn't say that. He mentioned that he'd been fired though. And his demands were pretty vague. He just didn't like the way the railroad treated its injured veterans."

"So was the bomb aimed at Charlotte to garner maximum attention?"

"He didn't say."

"It had to have been though, don't you think? Why else would it have been set on a timer to go off when she was there? I'm guessing that the bomber didn't want to kill her which is why they warned us."

Don't jump to that conclusion."

"Meaning what?"

"There was something about the note that struck me. I had a good look at it while we were waiting for the police. There was a high e on it. I mean the letter e was always higher on the page than the other letters, and just slightly on a rightward angle. It struck me that I'd seen this sort of thing before and then it came to me. I just had a look at the Charlotte Wyndham file from the foundation. Our correspondence was in it. When I looked at the typed letters I got back from Charlotte, accepting the contribution, and agreeing to the pick-up and drop-off schedules, I realized why the type on the bomber's letter looked familiar. I'm no expert but it sure looked like they'd both been typed on the same typewriter!" Victoria sounded … well, victorious.

"Geez. But Charlotte doesn't type anymore, I don't think. My understanding from when I was there is that Evelyn does all her typing for her."

"Exactly. I remembered you saying that. And I remembered you saying that everyone but Charlotte had telephones, so I called Evelyn."

"At first, Evelyn denied having had anything to do with the letter, but only at first," said Victoria. "She suddenly admitted it and said there was a reasonable explanation for the bomb, if you can imagine! She begged me not to say anything until she could explain in detail. I told her to go ahead but she said she wanted to show me something when she explained; like that would make everything clear. She asked to see me tomorrow. I promised I'd listen and keep quiet about things until then."

Victoria continued after a pause, "I can't believe she'll say anything that could ever make me turn against my father and let her get away with an attack on the railroad, and with blackmail, but I'll wait before I do anything else. ... So, we have a clandestine meeting set up." She laughed.

"So you aren't going to the cops but are meeting the bomber?" I said dubiously.

"Sounds dicey when you put it that way but I promised I wouldn't do anything til I met with her."

"What's her explanation? I wonder. She didn't say anything else?"

"Well, I mentioned that Charlotte could've been killed and Evelyn said that the bomb had been timed so people on the train would see the explosion and no one would be hurt; that's why that particular station was chosen, because no other passengers would be getting off except Charlotte. The great Charlotte Wyndham almost being killed would gain world wide attention. Evelyn said that she was supposed to be there to meet Charlotte so she planned to make sure they were nowhere near the bomb ... but she had a problem and didn't get there. It was for just such a possibility that her friend was on the train to tip you guys off. He was there as insurance so that no one would be hurt. Anyway, if I'm not entirely satisfied with what Evelyn says tomorrow morning I'll go see Charlotte when I come to Briggs the next day – what's that,

Thursday? – and I'll take Evelyn's letter to the Briggs' police to compare it to the bomber's note."

"Geez. Are you sure about this meeting?"

"It'll be fine. I'll call you from here, right after I talk to her, and let you know my plans."

After I hung up I thought of something. A real left field thought. I don't know where it came from except maybe from the photo of a suffragette I'd seen in a book at the library the evening before. It showed her, in pants, getting into a vehicle. In any case, I now wondered: was it possible that it hadn't actually been a man who'd warned us? Could it have been Evelyn dressed as a man? I know whispered voices, like the one that had warned me, are easily disguised, and before that the person had whistled, not sung. Maybe both were designed to mask her voice.

I had a bad feeling about Victoria's plan to meet Evelyn.

Editor's note: To expand on the earlier comment about film. Trains are a moving world detached from specific locales where we are constantly interacting with strangers.

As a result of wars, the dislocation of communities, the displacement of people, propaganda, and the spread of media, fear of the other – because of our solipsistic nature; that we cannot know the internal realities of others or even know if they exist – came to the fore. This dread consumes us appears in films and fiction. Fear of the other supplants past fears, such as the unnatural (werewolves), science (Frankenstein), and religion (Satan), as our chief source of anxiety.

It was the death of reality itself and the intensification of a world of simulation.

The suspense of Alfred Hitchcock's films, and of film noir, with its darkness and shadows that mirror a potential inner darkness in others, "developed during and after World War II, taking advantage of the post-war ambiance of anxiety, pessimism, and suspicion,"[30] drew from the anxiety of an existential dilemma due to our solipsism.

Hitchcock (and others) set suspense films on trains where uncertainty about identity and reality was at the heart of the story. Train passengers in *The Lady Vanishes* insist that a woman who was seen does not actually exist. *North By Northwest* is based on a case of mistaken identity. And *Strangers on a Train* (the perfect metaphor of the modern world) involves two men uncertain of themselves, one of whom is torn between two women and two lives.

Because a train stirs fears of the danger of being alone, and of not knowing who surrounds us (unlike what would be found in a community, where we know our neighbours), it also stirs fears of uncertain morality, of whether the norms we take for granted are in effect.

In the film *Strangers on a Train,* for example, the action revolves around the question of whether an average Joe can be convinced to murder someone.

---

30 Tim Dirks. amc filmsite. http://www.filmsite.org/filmnoir.html

We see these elements nicely utilized in (the non-Hitchcock book and film) *Murder on the Orient Express* where almost a whole train car of decent, upright people (stuck in a snow drift in the middle of nowhere), with most of them hiding their identities, collude to murder someone pretending to be a person he isn't. Meanwhile, the staunch defender of law and order, detective Hercule Poirot, ferrets them out through psychology (i.e. the soothing, supposed ability to genuinely know what goes on inside another's head) but becomes complicit with the murderers and helps them to evade the law, thus condoning their vigilante murder.

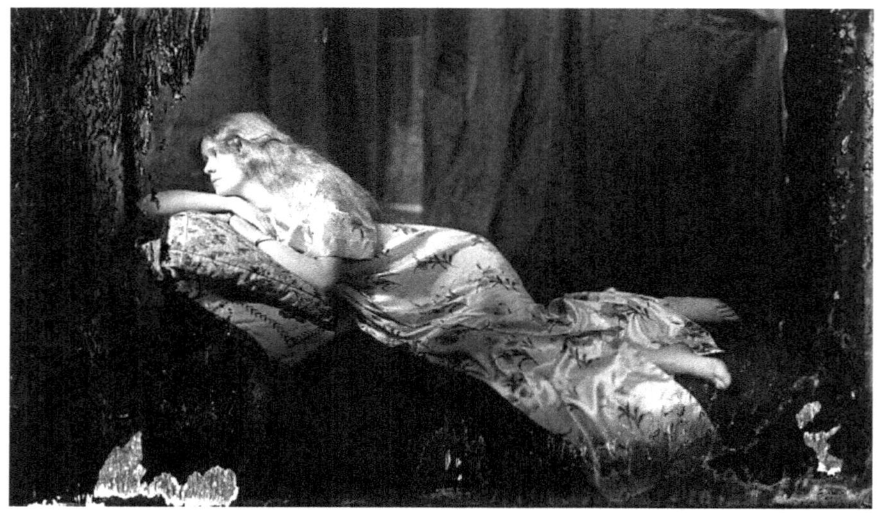

Next day, I waited all morning for Victoria's call. Nothing. Impatient, I eventually rang her after lunch. The maid answered and when I asked to speak to Victoria there was a long pause. I knew something bad was coming. I could hear it in the maid's voice. She finally started to cry and said, "I know who you are. You're her friend." And then she told me that Victoria had tried to commit suicide.

I was shocked, feeling disbelief and deja vu because of my sister. "You said 'tried,'" I eventually half yelled at her. "Is Victoria okay?"

"I don't know." She struggled for words. "I found her unconscious and right now she's in the hospital. I can't understand. She was happy in the morning. She went out for a while, came back, went to her room and changed her clothes. She then came down to the study. I thought she was going to use the phone when she closed the door. A little later I called her for lunch and when she didn't come I went in and found her on the floor unconscious. The ambulance man said it looked like she'd taken some pills. She was barely alive."

I didn't even tell anyone I was leaving work. I fled outside and grabbed a taxi to the train station. Luckily I only had a half hour wait for a train heading east, I don't know if I could've stood it much longer. I was striding around, frustrated at the wait and from not knowing what was happening with Victoria.

By the time I was on the train I was able to focus and think a little bit. I would call the cops when I got there, I thought. This had to be Evelyn's work. No wonder she'd wanted to see Victoria in person. Probably stole some drug from the hospital where she volunteered.

Suicide attempt! No bloody way. Maybe I wouldn't call the cops, I thought. If Victoria didn't recover I'd deal with Evelyn personally and there'd be no need to ever call them.

There was now no reason to believe that the bomb hadn't

been meant to kill. If Evelyn had attempted to fatally poison Victoria then murder was obviously within her capabilities.

I was suddenly convinced that the bomb had indeed been meant for Charlotte. Perhaps Evelyn wanted to inherit her land. It all fit. Evelyn had been 'late' so Charlotte would've been right beside the bomb when it went off. Evelyn had sent a note implicating a railroad employee and the person singing *Casey Jones* perhaps did so to reinforce this suggestion, that is, if I survived to tell the story. He or she might've been hiding at the station and had not even been on the train.

Or maybe, or even likely, Charlotte had been right when she suggested that there had been no warning, that what I'd heard was someone gloating. Something sinister.

I'd been so absorbed by these matters, since leaving my rooms, that I was unaware I was being followed. Or, that the person following had sat directly behind me on the train. I'd glanced in his direction when he got on ahead of me. He was nondescript, fortyish. I didn't recognize him. Later, I wouldn't have been able to provide a description of him if asked.

My fingers grip the handhold, and my feet land on the steps with sharp violence.

Still subject to raging adrenaline and needing to rid myself of some of its effects, I got up and walked through the train till I was out on the back deck of the caboose. I took hold of a rail with my right hand and looked at the forest rushing by beside me. I recognized the terrain. There was a town coming up where the train would soon stop.

The side view from a train renders reality a blur because of speed. Your senses aren't equipped for such unnatural speed. This was like my life right then as I struggled to grasp and make sense of the morning's events.

I heard the rear door of the caboose open behind me and glanced over my shoulder to see the man who'd been sitting behind me. I nodded and turned back to the scenery.

That's when the shove from behind knocked me off the train. My legs no longer found a solid substance under me. They waved behind the train.

My right-handed grip on the handhold had instinctively tightened and I twisted round managing to take hold of it with my left hand. The toes of my shoes bounced off the stony ground below before the wind, again carried them out behind me.

Using all my strength I pulled one leg forward. I was dangling from the side of the train so there were steps to my left. I swung my left leg around the end of the railing to get it on the steps.

At that moment, the man above began to punch and kick at me. My face, my chest, and then my hands. He swore loudly and yelled at me to let go.

I knew in an instant that I was facing the man I'd encountered on the platform of Cardew Station the night of the bomb. He was determined to kill me. I leaned back so that I could kick back at the guy. I kept thinking, 'Hold on, just for a bit!' I knew the train would begin to slow very soon, as it pulled into town.

Fortunately, I was younger and stronger than my opponent. I got lucky and landed a kick that knocked him backward. He grabbed hold of the railing.

I scrambled back up on to the deck.

I heard the train whistle and felt the sensation of slowing. I let go of the railing, stepped forward and swung at the man, making contact. He went backward and now he was the one in danger of going over.

I grabbed hold of his shirt front, and attempted to pull him back up on to the deck. But he went back to kicking out at me. He must have also felt the rapid slowing of the train because he was trying to get off.

And then he was on the ground, tumbling.

I watched him and resisted the urge to go after him.

He was soon up on his knees facing me, just a receding figure growing smaller.

Editor's note: The author's theory, that blurred scenery is a modern phenomena because our primitive senses can't cope with speed, is questionable. (Although this might be a metaphor regarding the effects of societal changes in the modern world.) Blur is common. Leibniz argued that, in blur, we actually perceive all of the composite pictures. As to the modern world, isn't it more likely that blur is something we get when we try to apprehend the world with technology? Distortion is often there only when perception is mediated. Many certainly don't see blur when looking at a moving train. I don't. (Again the author's veracity is in question.) But when we photograph it we see blur because it is an attempt to show movement with a technology meant to deny it. Our brains aren't cameras but part of a dynamic universe. They are honest to some degree, but photos lie.

I came face to face with Victoria's parents in the waiting room at the end of the hall where her room was located. I asked how she was.

They didn't seem to find my being there odd. John told me that his daughter had been revived a few hours before, but was weakened so the nurses had sent them here to let her recover some strength. He muttered about his confusion at her "suicide attempt".

Right then, a nurse came to advise John and Maxine that they may as well leave and return after dinner because Victoria was asleep.

So they left. I was invited to their house for dinner but declined, saying I had too much energy to burn off and wasn't hungry. I wanted to go for a walk instead.

And that's what I did.

I got back to the hospital at one minute before seven p.m. when visiting hours were to begin. No parents in the waiting room.

I walked straight to Victoria's room and no one tried to stop me. Expecting to see her parents there I stuck my head through the open door hoping for permission to go in.

Victoria was by herself and awake. She waved me forward.

I hugged her and asked how she was.

"Recovering. A little weak. What are you doing here?"

"Came to see how you were."

At that moment in time Evelyn, and what had happened, weren't at the forefront of my thoughts. But Victoria soon brought them up, explaining her morning. She'd gone to a tea room with Evelyn who must have put a drug into her tea. The overdose had been life threatening.

I shook my head, frowning and began to respond when Victoria continued.

"She brought some photos of a man with three kids. Said she'd met him at a hospital where she volunteers. He's been suffering with psychological problems resulting from the war. She said he'd been fired by the railroad, lost his income, health insurance, and was in danger of losing his kids. And that's why she was angry at K&L and wanted to hurt them."

"Did you believe her? I mean, maybe not about the man, but that she was out to hurt the railroad? Because alternately the plan could have been to kill Charlotte and inherit her estate; but to make it look like the unions had set the bomb. After all, she's just shown she's capable of murder. Even if what she said is true, about the man being in desperate straits, one could still make the case that she was trying to get Charlotte's money."

"It didn't occur to me at the time but it's what I was just thinking when you came in. It was pretty clear from what Evelyn said that she's in love with this fellow. After her little speech she asked me if I was going to the police or to Charlotte. I said I'd speak to my father because it was a railroad building that was destroyed and he deserved to know that the unions weren't involved. It was up to him what happened next. I wonder if that's the moment that Evelyn decided she'd have to kill me to protect herself and her friend."

"Did you tell her that you'd told me about her having written the letter?"

"Yes." Victoria looked at me with surprise. "She began pressing me with so many questions about whether I'd told anyone about our meeting that I began to get a little nervous and thought I'd be safer if she thought someone else knew. Why?"

"Her partner tried to kill me."

Victoria sat up, alarmed. "I'm sorry," she said incredulously.

"No, no," I cut her off. "It's not your fault." I glanced towards the door.

Victoria read my mind. "My parents should be here soon. I'll get my father to call the police. Fortunately I still have Evelyn's typed correspondence with the wonky letter c."

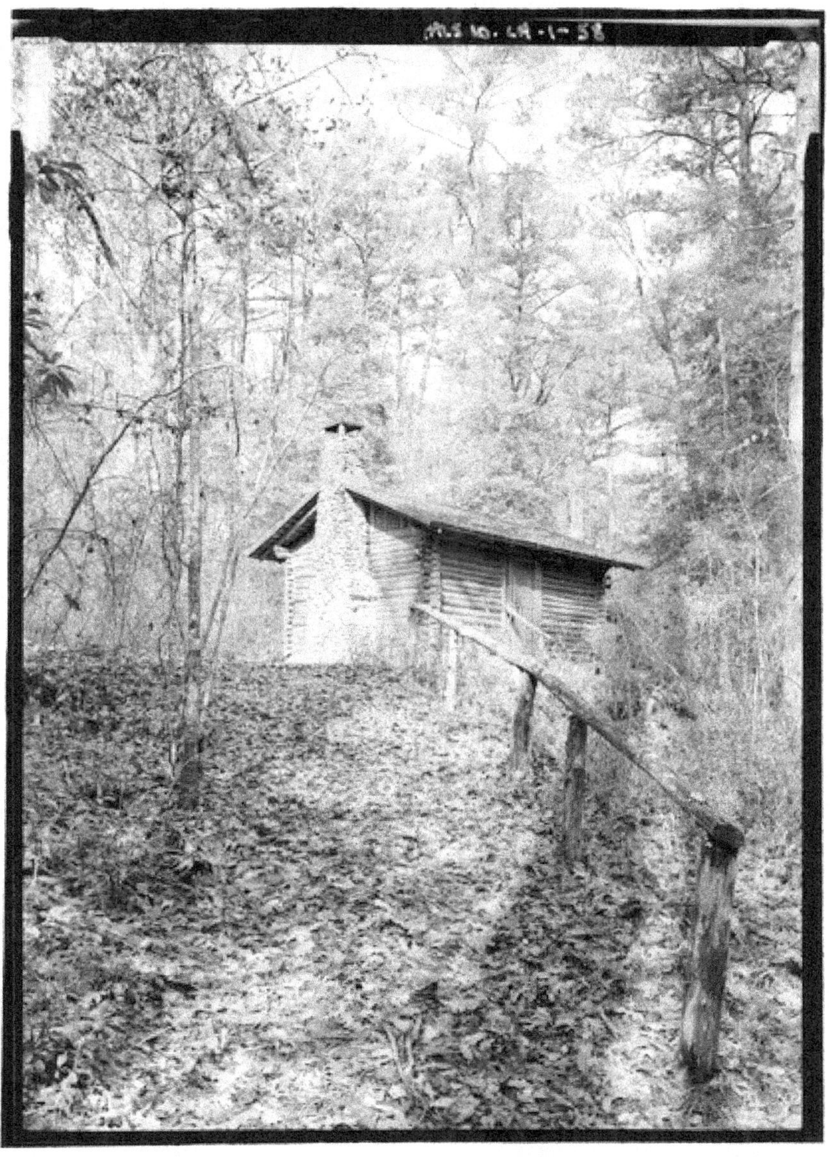

I was up first thing next morning and arrived at Charlotte's around seven a.m. with the intention of filling her in on what Victoria had told me; if the police hadn't already done so. And my own theories. I assumed the police would've already taken Evelyn away and Charlotte would be frantic.

The police were still there. There were two cruisers in front of Evelyn's house.

I walked to Charlotte's and saw her sitting on the front step of the cabin, being interviewed.

She nodded at me and held up a finger in a "be with you in a minute" sign.

I pointed towards the cliffs behind her cabin and she nodded.

As I trudged along I thought about the warning I'd heard at the train station.

"Mounted to the cabin with his orders in his hand
And he took his farewell trip to that Promised Land."

I was now certain that the singing was a sign of utter callousness; a glorying in the death of people who'd done nothing to hurt the singer. Folks he didn't even know. I'd only figured out its import because I subconsciously recognized that the man running was fleeing for his life. I'd seen enough of that in the war.

I walked along the circumference of the cliff for fifty yards or so before stopping to look out at the majestic scene of lake and islands spread before me down below. I heard a noise behind and turned.

Not five feet away stood Evelyn's partner in crime, watching me. His face was badly scraped; I assume from the tumble off the train the day before.

"I came to see Evelyn," he said quietly. "She's gone." He sounded bewildered.

I edged slightly to my right to get a tree between myself and the cliff's edge. "I assume she's been arrested for trying to kill Victoria Spires and maybe Charlotte Wyndham," I said.

He sighed. "It's my fault. She was only trying to help me. To get this property and sell it to a developer. And … What do you think'll happen?"

"It's two attempted murders. It could be bad." I studied him for a moment. "Is what Evelyn told Victoria true, that you have kids and lost your job?"

"Yes."

"Then you might consider turning yourself in. It's mitigating circumstances I would think."

"But then I'll go to jail and what'll my kids have? They already lost their mother."

"Don't you have any other family?"

"None that I want near my kids … I can't go to jail." It was said as a statement of fact but belligerence and anger had emerged in the man's tone of voice.

"But the police will come for you."

"Why would they do that? No one knows about my connection to Evelyn. She won't give me up. Cops'll be looking for someone who got turfed from the railroad but that was a lie Evelyn made up. It was the power company. Not that Spires treated his employees any better than them. But the railroad story was just a ruse to hide the motive. It's only you who knows."

Yes, I knew. I watched his face as he grasped the import of the statement. His face twisted in rage and he snorted, I swear, like a bull. And then he charged.

It was a clumsy and furious foray. I merely stepped aside. He brushed off me and would've gone over the cliff except I grabbed his arm and yanked him back.

It was an anti-climax. I threw him on the ground, sat on to his chest to pin him and began to yell for the cops while he struggled.

They took their sweet time getting there.

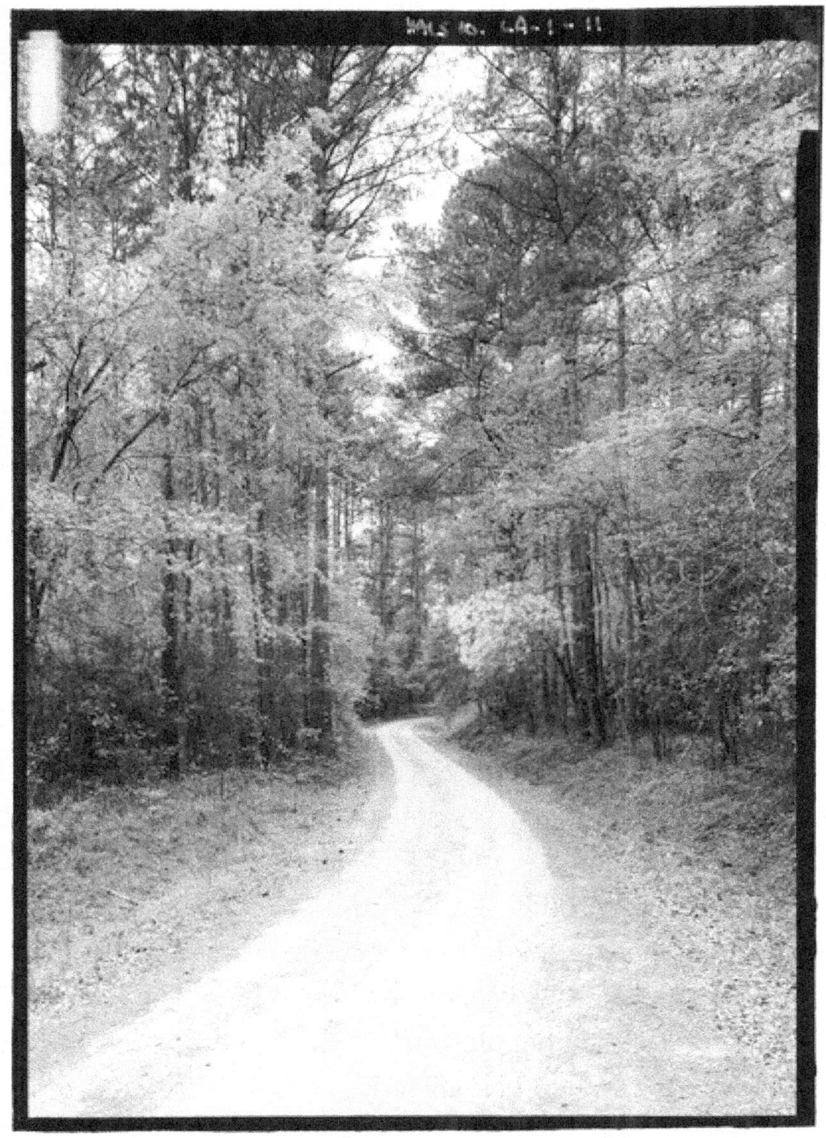

It was three days later before I finally had the chance to sit down with Charlotte Wyndham.

She told me she'd been to visit Evelyn in jail.

"I feel sorry for her," Charlotte said. "She met her

accomplice while working at the hospital. He was struggling in every way and broke. But she came to love him. And she wanted money to help him. The old story. Poverty and desperation with no end in sight leads to crime. I think she got the idea to implicate the unions from the suffragette stories I told her, about using explosions for publicity."

I said, "Did he put Evelyn up to it?"

"I don't know. I think it was likely more complicated than that; something that just evolved out of frustration and anger. It spawned hate. I became expendable to Evelyn in order to save the man she loved. So she acted out of a new loyalty that overcame the old. Maybe the money was also about a chance at her having a life. Both of them had experienced the death of their first great love and never formed a strong attachment with anyone else after that, until they met each other."

"I didn't know that about Evelyn. I thought she had a good life here."

"Her young man died in that unnecessary first world war when she was twenty-one. I don't think she ever got over it, the pain just lingered. Likely why she tried to help injured soldiers this time around. I'd like to think she had a good life here but I suppose it might have just been an escape from the world. In the last few years she'd become re-engaged with society, was meeting people. I think she began to miss having money; money for clothes and nice things. She liked those. You can't live the life here without choosing it. Unless it's what you really want, you'll just feel deprived."

Because of what Evelyn and her partner had done, we knew they'd obviously be in jail for the foreseeable future. Charlotte said she'd send enough money to help his kids – helping orphans was where much of her money went anyway

– but they would still grow up without any parents.

She got up and slowly walked across the room. She looked at a framed photo, the famous one of her from 1880 and the only photo in the room.

"I should get rid of this," she said. "This, and my own longing for the past. You think photos help you hold on to life, and defy death, but death is just a part of life. The young man I was thinking about at the moment the photo was taken knew that and accepted death. A photo isn't life. It freezes things. It's closer to the truth to say that they kill life and make ghosts to haunt us. They say, 'This moment is somehow more significant than any other, that life is these moments and the rest is filler'. Which is nonsense. Life shouldn't be seen like that."

And that's when she gave me the famous photo and, of course, I'll forever think of Charlotte when I see it.

Editor's note: Evelyn Carter received a ten year prison sentence while her lover and accomplice, Elliot Turner, got five years. They eventually reunited and disappeared from view.

It emerged during their trials that, after meeting at the hospital, the two began to attend a local non-denominational church at the urging of Turner. This was the church run by the notorious Dusan A. Dusan, a charismatic messiah wannabe who convinced people to kill for him. His followers feared and adored him.

Neither Evelyn nor Elliot claimed the influence of Dusan as a mitigating factor in their actions, although this has often been speculated on. Others (who maybe don't like open-endedness or who have some personal agenda) have argued that Elliot's financial condition and Evelyn's desire to overcome her own sense of deprivation are sufficient explanation for what they did.

Famously, Dusan was tracked down and killed in a fire fight by the notorious actress Devlin Kira on behalf of a former follower who Dusan had ordered to kill his own first born as punishment for the man's doubting him, as recounted in her book, *Faust and the Dragon Lady* (so called because of her red hair and rosacea).

Devlin Kira later went into hiding. Rumors persist that she never existed, yet several photos purporting to be images of Devlin have surfaced over the years – as if that proves she's real.

Endnote

To write this story I compiled several thematic pools of creative commons images (trains, 1946, suffragettes, young women wearing white, the city, the country, etc. and a few one-offs that I liked as well) from the Wikimedia Commons and Library of Congress internet sites. The themes were random, selected because I saw multiple images of a subject.

I had no story in mind when I began to write; it was entirely automatic. I would select an image from the pools that I felt could advance the story and then write to it. Each image used suggested the next step in the story.

All characters are fictitious. The images are not illustrations. The people depicted are not the characters in the book; even if it is suggested in the text that they might be. No commentary on the character of the actual subjects of these photos is intended by their use. Rod Dubey even writes in the guise of a certain type of editor. It is all lies.

Rosina Plumley

Photo Credits

The following images are listed as having no known copyright restrictions at the locations cited.

Preface. 'Curtis, Oklahoma. Helper engine leaving the train on Atchison, Topeka, and Santa Fe Railroad.' Jack Delano. No known copyright restrictions.
http://www.loc.gov/pictures/item/owi2001021488/PP/
Page 5. 'Woman reading, about 1890 National Media Museum - Kodak Gallery Collection.' National Media Museum, UK. No known copyright restrictions.
http://commons.wikimedia.org/wiki/
File:Woman_reading_(2780164461).jpg?uselang=en-ca
Page 25. 'Wood-nymph.' Frances Benjamin Johnston. No known restrictions on publication.
http://www.loc.gov/pictures/collection/fbj/item/96503522/
Page 48. 'The far west - shooting buffalo on the line of the Kansas-Pacific Railroad / Bghs.' Library of Congress.
http://www.loc.gov/pictures/item/2004669992/
Page 72. 'Four Dancing Figures.' Frances Benjamin Johnston.
http://www.loc.gov/pictures/collection/fbj/item/2002698065/
Page 79. "Red Maples," Mrs. Rosina Sherman Hoyt House, Southampton, New York. 'Pavilion overlooking lily pool.' Library of Congress.
http://www.loc.gov/pictures/collection/fbj/item/2008675748/
Page 81. "Red Maples," Mrs. Rosina Sherman Hoyt House, Southampton, New York. 'Stairway to sunken garden.' Library of Congress.
http://www.loc.gov/pictures/collection/fbj/item/2008675749/
Page 83. '"Red Maples," Mrs. Rosina Sherman Hoyt House, Southampton, New York. 'Herbaceous garden and entrance to hedge garden.' Library of Congress.
http://www.loc.gov/pictures/collection/fbj/item/2008675714/

Page 109. Cropped image. 'Original glass plate negative is from the J. C. Knowles Collection, PhC.182, State Archives of North Carolina.'

http://tinyurl.com/yaape83y

Page 117. Cropped image. 'Original glass plate negative is from the J. C. Knowles Collection, PhC.182, State Archives of North Carolina.'

http://tinyurl.com/y94x9rk2

Page 126. Six dancing figures.' Frances Benjamin Johnston.

http://www.loc.gov/pictures/collection/fbj/item/2002698064/

 *The following images are listed as public domain at the locations cited.*

Cover. This image has been cropped. 1914. 'Soldiers leave for war, Union Station. (Toronto, Canada).' William James. City of Toronto Archives.

https://commons.wikimedia.org/wiki/
File:Soldiers_leave_for_war_at_Union_Station_Toronto.jpg

Frontispiece and Page 77. 'Original glass plate negative is from the J. C. Knowles Collection, PhC.182, State Archives of North Carolina.'

http://tinyurl.com/ycztw87t

Page 7. 'Rural Bank welcome home party.' Sam Hood. The State Library of New South Wales
collection.

http://tinyurl.com/o6hbfg8

Page 9. 'Rain, Steam and Speed - The Great Western Railway.' J.M.W. Turner. National Gallery.

http://tinyurl.com/ycy7dlkt

Page 11. 'Chicago, Illinois. A Chicago, Milwaukee, Saint Paul, and Pacific Railroad train, just arrived at Union Station, 1943.' Jack Delano.

https://commons.wikimedia.org/wiki/

File:Chicago,_Illinois_by_Jack_Delano_1943.jpg

Page 13. *The Great Train Robbery*, N.C. Wyeth. 'English: painting to illustrate McKeon's Graft a story by Luke Thrice (real name John Riussell) published in the periodical New Story Magazine, vol. IV, no. 6. 1912, The painting was the cover of the issue.

https://commons.wikimedia.org/wiki/File:Greattrainrobbery.jpg

Page 15. Cropped image showing unidentified girl in an art class at the Newcastle Technical College Art School. Sam Hood. The State Library of New South Wales collection.

http://tinyurl.com/ojurajw

Page 17. 'Rural Bank welcome home party.' Sam Hood. The State Library of New South Wales

 collection.

http://tinyurl.com/nexzxrf

Page 20. Still from 'Rail Strike Paralyzes Entire U.S., 1946/05/23.' Universal Studios.

https://archive.org/details/1946-05-

23_Rail_Strike_Paralyzes_Entire_US

Page 23. 'Arlington, Virginia. Girls entertaining their guests in one of the two card rooms, at a residence for the women who work in the U.S. government for the duration of the war. More privacy is afforded here than in the main lounge.' Esther Bubley for the Office of War Information.

http://tinyurl.com/oe59exv

Page 28. 'View of Ford Mansion's second floor hallway looking towards the main bedroom -

Richmond Hill Plantation, Ford Mansion, East of Richmond Hill on Ford Neck Road, Richmond Hill, Bryan County, GA.' Historic American Buildings Survey.

http://tinyurl.com/pyzyc44

Page 29. 'Men (and a woman), probably commuters, walking along a platform next to a train in Chicago, Illinois. The near car is probably a "Blue-series" sleeping car from Pullman-Standard, manufactured by Pullman-Standard for the Super Chief in 1947-

1948. Each "Blue-series" had 10 roomettes, 2 compartments and 3 double bedrooms.' Stanley Kubrick.

http://tinyurl.com/nbdm34l

Page 31. "Moving up through Prato, Italy, men of the 370th Infantry Regiment, have yet to climb the mountain which lies ahead." Bull, April 9, 1945.' U.S. National Archives and Records Administration.

http://commons.wikimedia.org/wiki/

File:Ww2_allied_advance_prato_italy.jpg?uselang=en-ca

Page 34. 'Photo of a high school girl, a student at Woodrow Wilson High School, Washington, DC.' Esther Bubley for the Office of War Information.

http://tinyurl.com/pchb42q

Page 37. 'Postcard photo of The Mountaineer in service. The train was originally named Flying Yankee and assumed this name and route in summers from 1942 to 1952.' L.L. Cook Co., Milwaukee.

http://commons.wikimedia.org/wiki/

File:Boston_and_Maine_Railroad_The_Mountaineer.JPG

Page 39. 'Explosion of a napalm bomb in Korea, dropped by a U.S. Navy Douglas AD-4N Skyraider of Composite Squadron VC-35 Det.F "Night Hecklers". VC-35 Det.F was assigned to Carrier Air Group 101 (CVG-101) aboard the aircraft carrier USS Kearsarge (CVA-33) for a deployment to Korea from 11 August 1952 to 17 March 1953.' U.S. Navy.

http://tinyurl.com/qceog8t

Page 42. 1953 Ogatsutama powder mill explosion. 'Outer clothes etc. of employees scattered on site.'

http://tinyurl.com/pwkeek4

Page 43. 'News stand at the southwest corner St. Andrew Street and Spadina Avenue, Toronto, Ontario, Canada.' City of Toronto Department of Public Works.

http://tinyurl.com/no4rnfd

Page 45. 'Steam locomotives of the Chicago & North Western Railway in the roundhouse at the Chicago, Illinois rail yards.' Jack

Delano.

http://en.wikipedia.org/wiki/File:Locomotives-Roundhouse2.jpg

Page 50. 'Switchman throwing a switch at Chicago and Northwest Railway Company's Proviso yard, Chicago, Illinois.' Jack Delano.

http://tinyurl.com/yasp5cqt

Page 53. 'Chicago, Illinois. In the waiting room of the Union Station.' Jack Delano.

http://commons.wikimedia.org/wiki/

File:Chicago_Union_Station_1943.jpg?uselang=en-ca

Page 55. 1939. Unknown photographer. Fortepan.

http://tinyurl.com/ybasbqkt

Page 58. Cropped image. 'An elderly patient at St. Elizabeth's Hospital in Washington, D.C.' Harris & Ewing Collection glass negative, Library of Congress.

http://tinyurl.com/yabv9jtq

Page 61. 'View of Writer's Cabin looking from the southeast - Briarwood- The Caroline Dormon Nature Preserve, 216 Caroline Dormon Road, Saline, Bienville Parish, LA.' James W. Rosenthal. ibrary of Congress Prints and Photographs Division Washington, D.C. 20540 USA.

http://tinyurl.com/o2r4u37

Page 64. 'War gardeners near Washington DC.' Library of Congress Harris and Ewing collection.

http://tinyurl.com/yabzu3jc

Page 66. 'Fireplace wall of east room - Isaac Small House, Old King's Highway and Highland Road, Truro, Barnstable County, MA.' Historic American Buildings Survey.

http://tinyurl.com/p9lnzgh

Page 69. 'Bedford Magazine Explosion blast cloud.' *The Other Halifax Explosion.*

http://tinyurl.com/yb34upwu

Page 74. 'German actress Hedwig Reicher wearing costume of "Columbia" with other suffrage pageant participants standing in background in front of the Treasury Building, March 3, 1913,

Washington, D.C. The pageant featured an allegory in which Columbia summoned Justice, Charity, Liberty, Peace, and Hope to review the new crusade of women.' Library of Congress George Grantham Bain Collection.

http://tinyurl.com/yal96tp3

Page 77. Cropped version of **Frontspiece,** see credit above.

Page 85. "'Commuters, who have just come off the train, waiting for the bus to go home, Lowell, Mass.' Jack Delano.

http://tinyurl.com/ydbnkl78

Page 88. 'Photo shows two people walking along road near a billboard that says "Next time, try the train. Relax." Nitrate negative. 2 1/4 x 2 1/4 inches.' Dorothea Lange.

http://tinyurl.com/y9ywnnxf

Page 91. 'Switch engine in yard near Calumet Park stockyards, Indiana Harbor Belt Railroad. Calumet City, Illinois, January 1943.' Jack Delano.

http://tinyurl.com/nc2madf

Page 93. 'Store window of Simpsons Department Store, St. Catherine Street, Montreal, Canada.' Conrad Poirier.

http://tinyurl.com/y7qyvs9y

Page 95. 'A Visit To An Anti-aircraft Ship, England, 1940. An AB (Able Seaman) fuses a 4 inch shell whilst sitting on the 'grog tub' on board this anti-aircraft ship, England 1940.' Ministry of Information Photo Division Photographer.

http://tinyurl.com/ydelelz2

Page 98. 'Young Woman.' Albert Schickedanz. Private collection.

http://tinyurl.com/y9yypf7d

Page 101. 'Woman putting on her lipstick in a park with Union Station behind her, Washington, D.C.' Library of Congress.

http://tinyurl.com/nsn32zx

Page 103. "'Bethlehem graveyard and steel mill, Pennsylvania," by the American photographer Walker Evans, nitrate negative, 8 inches x 10 inches. Dated November 1935.'

http://tinyurl.com/ndm2wx5

Page 105. 'A young worker at the C & NW RR 40th Street shops, Chicago, Ill.' Jack Delano.

http://tinyurl.com/obvwzyc

Page 107. 'African American man going in "colored" entrance of movie house on Saturday afternoon, Belzoni, Mississippi Delta, Mississippi' Marion Post Wolcott.

http://tinyurl.com/y8bkccrd

Page 112. 'Woman showing a marching costume, Chicago suffrage parade, June 6, 1916 (tight-fitting trousers under skirts, which preserved technical modesty, but would have been considered unacceptably masculinized by many at the time).' Bain Collection.

http://tinyurl.com/y7gfwa4j

Page 115. 'The irritating gentleman.' 1874. Berthold Woltze.

http://tinyurl.com/ycp5nqrh

Page 118. 'Streetcars in front of Union Station, Toronto, Canada.' Canadian Museum of Science and Technology, Canadian National Collection.

http://tinyurl.com/qdxwsjb

Page 120. 'An illustration from "Holding Her Down" by Jack London, that shows an episode from this story. Jack London jumps on a moving train.' From *The Road*, 1907.

http://tinyurl.com/ycsffoy8

Page 123. 'A Milan metro (subway / underground) train approaching a station - the slow shutter speed of the rather dark tunnel results in the train being somewhat blurred.' Spsmiler.

http://tinyurl.com/y7m62vq9

Page 124. 'Exterior view of Santa Fe Railroad Hospital, opposite Hollenbeck Park, in Boyle Heights, Los Angeles, 1905.' California Historical Society Collection.

http://tinyurl.com/nplxj8y

Page 128. 'View of Writer's Cabin (or Three Pines Cabin) and path looking from the southeast (similar to HALS no. LA-1-35) - Briarwood- The Caroline Dormon Nature Preserve, 216 Caroline Dormon Road, Saline, Bienville Parish, LA.' James W. Rosenthal. Library of Congress Prints and Photographs Division Washington, D.C. 20540 USA.

http://tinyurl.com/obrpy9x

Page 130. 'Lake from Eagle Cliff. Alternate Title: Lake Mohonk scenery.' J. Loeffler.

http://tinyurl.com/ydas79nd

Page 132. 'View in the Shagbark Hickory area looking north to the visitor's center (duplicate of HALS no. LA-1-2 (CT)) - Briarwood- The Caroline Dormon Nature Preserve, 216 Caroline Dormon Road, Saline, Bienville Parish, LA." James W. Rosenthal. Library of Congress Prints and Photographs Division Washington, D.C. 20540 USA.

http://tinyurl.com/nvxdewg

Page 135. Cropped image. 'Head Study (reclining woman in white blouse and blue skirt).' Sergei Prokudin-Gorskii.

http://tinyurl.com/yd66qt2l

Endnote. 'Emily Pierson Handing out Leaflets in New York State Suffrage Campaign, ca. 1915.' F.E. Redmond, Post-Standard, Syracuse, N.Y.

http://tinyurl.com/y925q9qq

Inconsequential Diversions

For information on Inconsequential Diversions visit:
https://inconsequentialdiversions.wordpress.com/

About the *raindrips to Rethfernhim Series*:

The novels in this series combine genre fiction with art, commentary, and photography. Meant to be art objects, they are ontological mysteries which focus on the death of reality.

Also in the *raindrips to Rethfernhim Series*:

The Japanese Fire Tree
by Rosina Plumley

"It seemed that the war on art was still on."

While Blanche Christie sits in jail looking at certain conviction—the unwitting victim of a scam to steal 'The Japanese Fire Tree', a valuable Egon Schiele painting owned by a wealthy American collector—her friends concoct an audacious scheme to set her free.

The Japanese Fire Tree is a novel

The Japanese Fire Tree is a satire of the art world

The Japanese Fire Tree is a multi-media montage including disintegrating art

The Japanese Fire Tree is an art object

The Japanese Fire Tree is an indictment of contemporary America – 1984 redux

The Japanese Fire Tree is full of fakes and fakers

The Japanese Fire Tree is a handbook for street art activists